Frederick Ross

Legendary Yorkshire

Frederick Ross

Legendary Yorkshire

ISBN/EAN: 9783337153205

Printed in Europe, USA, Canada, Australia, Japan

Cover: Foto ©Andreas Hilbeck / pixelio.de

More available books at **www.hansebooks.com**

BY

FREDERICK ROSS, F.R.H.S.,

AUTHOR OF

"CELEBRITIES OF YORKSHIRE WOLDS," "YORKSHIRE FAMILY ROMANCE,"
ETC.

HULL:

WILLIAM ANDREWS & CO., THE HULL PRESS.

LONDON : SIMPKIN, MARSHALL, HAMILTON, KENT, & CO., LIMITED.

1892.

NOTE.

Contents.

LEGENDARY YORKSHIRE.

The Enchanted Cave.

WHO is there that has not heard of the famous and redoubtable hero of history and romance, Arthur, King of the British, who so valiantly defended his country against the pagan Anglo-Saxon invaders of the island? Who has not heard of the lovely but frail Guenevera, his Queen, and the galaxy of female beauty that constituted her Court at Caerleon? Who has not heard of his companions-in-arms—the brave and chivalrous Knights of the Round Table, who went forth as knights-errant to succour the weaker sex, deliver the oppressed, liberate those who had fallen into the clutches of enchanters, giants, or malicious dwarfs, and especially in quest of the Holy Graal, that mystic chalice, in which were caught the last drops of blood of the expiring Saviour,

A

and which, in consequence, became possessed of wondrous properties and marvellous virtue of a miraculous character?

If such there be, let him lose no time in perusing Sir John Mallory's "La Morte d' Arthur," the "Chronicles of Geoffrey of Monmouth," the "Mabinogian of the Welsh," or the more recent "Idylls of the King," of Tennyson. According to Nennius, after vanquishing the Saxons in many battles, he crossed the sea, and carried his victorious arms into Scotland, Ireland, and Gaul, in which latter country he obtained a decisive victory over a Roman army. Moreover, that during his absence Mordred, his nephew, had seduced his queen and usurped his government, and that in a battle with the usurper, in 542, at Camlan, in Cornwall, he was mortally wounded; was conveyed to Avalon (Glastonbury), where he died of his wound, and was buried there. It is also stated that in the reign of Henry II. his reputed tomb was opened, when his bones and his magical sword "Excaliber" were found. This is given on the authority of Giraldus Cambrensis, who informs us that he was present on the occasion. But the popular belief in the West of England was that he did not die as represented, his soul having entered the body of a raven, which it will inhabit until he reappears to deliver England in some great extremity of peril.

This is what is told us by old chroniclers of Western England, the Welsh bards, and some romance writers; but in Yorkshire we have a different version of the story. It is true, say our legends, that Arthur was a mighty warrior, the greatest and most valiant that the island of Britain has produced either before or since; a man, moreover, of the most devout chivalry and gentle courtesy, and withal so pure in his life and sincere in his piety as a Christian, that he alone is worthy to find the Holy Graal, if not in his former life, in that which is forthcoming for he is not dead, but reposes in a spell-bound sleep, along with his knights, Sir Launcelot, Sir Gawaine, Sir Perceval, etc., and that the time is coming when the needs of England will be such as only his victorious arm, wielding his magically wrought Excaliber, can rescue from irretrievable ruin. He sleeps—it is asserted—along with his knights, in a now undiscoverable cavern beneath the Castle of Richmond, whence he will issue in the fulness of time, scatter the enemies of

England like chaff before the wind, as he so frequently dispersed the hordes of Teuton pagans, and place England on a higher eminence among the nations of the earth than it has ever previously attained. This enchanted cave has been seen but once, and by one man only. It happened in this wise :—

Once on a time there dwelt in Richmond one Peter Thompson. At what period he flourished is not recorded, but it matters not, although a little trouble in searching the parish registers and lists of burgesses of the town might reveal the fact. He gained a living by the fabrication of earthenware, and hence was popularly known amongst his comrades and townspeople as Potter Thompson. He was a simple and meek-minded man, small in stature and slender in limb, never troubling himself with either general or local politics. His voice was never heard at the noisy meetings of the vestry, nor did he join in the squabbles attendant on the meetings of the electors for the choice of their municipal governors or representatives in Parliament; he merely recorded his vote for the candidate who came forward as the representative of the colour he supported, leaving the shouting and quarrelling and cudgel-playing to those of his fellow-townsmen who had a liking for such rough work. As for himself, he was only too glad when he had discharged his duty as a citizen to get back to his clay and his wheel, for he was an industrious little fellow, had plenty of work, and was thus enabled, by living a frugal life, to lay by a little money, and would have lived a comfortable and happy life but for one circumstance.

Unfortunately, Peter Thompson was a married man; not that matrimony, in the abstract, is a misfortune, but he was unfortunate inasmuch as his wife was a termagant, and made his life miserable. Her tongue went clack, clack, clacking all day long; nothing that he did was right. She declared herself to be the greatest fool in Richmond to have united herself to an insignificant little wretch like him; and even when the bed curtains were drawn around them at night, the poor fellow was kept awake for an hour or more while she dinned into his ears a lecture on his manifold faults and his failures of duty as a husband. Peter seldom replied, but bore it all with meekness, and allowed her to go on with her monologue until she was tired, or ceased for want of breath. At times, when she was more exasperating than usual, he would start up from his wheel, clap his hat on his head, and rush out of the house to escape her pertinacious scolding. At such times he would go wandering about the hills and picturesque scenery by which Richmond is environed, and especially about the hill on which stands the Castle, and amongst the castle ruins, remaining away for three or four hours, moodily meditating on the mischance or infatuation which had led him to ally himself with so untoward a helpmate.

It chanced one day that Peter, unable to endure the persecution of his wife's tongue, rushed out of his house with the full intention of throwing himself into the Swale, so as to end his misery there and then. It was a brilliant summer's day, and there was a glorious sheen cast over hill and vale, rock and ravine, the silvery river winding between its emerald-hued banks and the clumps of foliaged woodland— over the Castle keep standing pre-eminently above all other buildings, church tower, ruined friary, antique bridge, and the quaint houses of the burghers, with the tower of Easby gleaming in the distance, imparting to the whole scene,

which is one of the most picturesque in Yorkshire
—which is saying a great deal, and which for
natural beauty can scarcely be surpassed in
England—a charm which had a wonderful effect
on Peter's perturbed mind. He was a lover of
nature in all her aspects, and an ardent admirer
of the landscape beauties which surrounded his
native town; and he began to reflect, as he ran
down the slope, that if he carried out his purpose,
he would never more be able to delight his eyes
with the lovely prospects of nature so lavishly
displayed before him at that moment; and by
the time he reached the river's bank he had
almost determined to live on and find com-
pensation for his domestic discomforts in his
communings with nature—or at least, continued
he to himself—"I will take another turn among
the hills and rocks and old ivy-mantled ruins,
before I bid good-bye to it all." He wandered
along round the base of the Castle hill, his spirits
becoming more elevated the farther he went, as
he gazed on the glorious landscape which
gradually became revealed to his view. Anon he
fell into a contemplative mood, and reasoned
calmly and philosophically on the wisdom of
disregarding the minor ills of life, when it was

possible for him as a compensating alternative to revel in the delights he was now enjoying, and he soon forgot altogether his purpose of terminating his woes and his life together from the parapet of Swale bridge. Onward he wandered; when suddenly turning a corner he came upon a spot altogether unknown to him—a ravine which seemed to wind away under the Castle hill, walled in with rugged rocks, from whose crevices sprang upward trees and shrubs, whilst underfoot was a flooring of rough scattered stones and fragments of fallen rocks, which appeared not to have been trodden for centuries. Astonished at the sight, for he imagined that he knew every nook in the neighbourhood, he rubbed his eyes to ascertain whether he was dreaming; but he found himself to be fully awake, and the unknown ravine to be a palpable reality. It just flashed across his mind that sorcery had been at work, and that what he beheld was the result of necromancy, for in his time enchanters, warlocks, wizards, and witches were rife in the land; but Peter had a bold heart, and he resolved upon solving the mystery by an exploration of the recesses of the ravine, let what would come of it.

Summoning up all his courage, Peter entered the

ravine, stumbling now and then over the stones bestrewn along his pathway. The road wound about, now to one side then to another, and the trees overhead to stretch out towards each other so as to overshadow the ravine and impart a twilight effect, which, as Peter proceeded onward, deepened into gloom, and eventually almost to darkness. At this period, when he was compelled to move along with caution, he encountered what at first seemed to be a wall of rock forming the end of the ravine. On feeling it carefully he found it to be a huge boulder which obstructed his path, but, his courage failing him not, he found means to clamber over it and land safely on the further side. On looking about him, as well as he could by the dim light, he found that he had alighted on the entrance to a cavern, the boulder seeming as if it had been placed there to prevent the intrusion of unauthorised persons, and then he imagined that it might be the cave of a gang of banditti, and was at once their treasure house and their refuge in times of peril; and this idea seemed to be confirmed by the circumstance that he could perceive, in the extreme distance, a glimmer of light. He felt that it would be extremely dangerous to be discovered in the purlieus of their haunt, but curiosity got the better of his fears, and he resolved upon going forward, mentally adding "After all it may be nothing more than the daylight streaming in at the other end, and by going on I may come out into the open air without having to return by the rough, shinbreaking road by which I have come;" and onward he went, feeling his way by the rocky walls cautiously and slowly, and, it must be added, with some degree of trepidation.

As he proceeded along, the distant light increased, and could be seen beaming through an opening like a doorway, with a mild effulgence resembling moonlight. Clearly it could not be the light of the sun streaming in through the aperture, and Peter, becoming more convinced that he was either approaching a robbers' haunt or a scene of enchantment, crept along as silently as possible, with some timidity, it is true; but having come thus far, and his curiosity being excited to the utmost pitch, he determined to carry out his adventure to the end. As he approached the portal, he stood to listen; but not the slightest sound broke the death-like stillness, and concluding from this that the cave was not

occupied—at least, was not at present he
ventured onward with silent footstep, and stood
within the illuminated aperture. What was his
amazement cannot be told at beholding the scene
before him. The opening gave entrance to a
lofty and spacious cavern, its walls glittering with
crystals and spars, whilst from the roof depended
a profusion of stalactites, glistening and scintilla-
ting with hues of spectroscopic brilliancy. The
light which was diffused around seemed to be
something supernatural; it was not that of the
sun, nor that of the moon, nor was it our modern
electric light; but seemed to be an intensity of
phosphoric radiance—soft, mild, and provocative of
slumber—which came not from any lamp or
other visible source, but appeared to be self-
evolved from the atmosphere. In the centre of
the cave, upon a rocky table or couch, lay the
figure of a kingly personage, resting his head on
his right hand, after the fashion of the recumbent
effigies in our mediæval churches. He was clad
in resplendent armour and a superb over-cloak,
with a golden crown, studded with precious
stones, encircling his head. By his side was a
circular shield emblazoned with arms, which
would have told Peter, had he been versed in

heraldry, that the owner was the famous King Arthur; whilst close by, suspended from the wall, were a diamond-hilted sword in a chased golden scabbard, and a highly ornamented horn, such as were used by military leaders for collecting their scattered troops. Around the King lay his twelve Knights of the Round Table, some prostrate on the floor, others reposing on fragments and projections of the rocks, each one handsome in figure and reclining in unstudied natural grace, presenting a study for a painter. They all lay as still as death save that their heaving chests and audible breathing showed that they were wrapped in profound slumber. Peter gazed upon them for a while with wondering eyes, keeping within the doorway, so as to have the road clear behind him for escape, in case of any hostile demonstration on the part of the knights. As they still slumbered on, without any sign of awakening, he plucked up courage enough to go amongst them; and, attracted by the splendour of the sword, he took it down to examine it more closely; then took it by the handle, and half drew it from its sheath. The moment he had done so, the sleepers around him gave symptoms of awakening, turned themselves, and seemed to be preparing to rise; but the spell of disenchantment was not complete. Peter, terribly alarmed at what he saw, pushed back the sword into the scabbard, threw it on the floor, and hurried with all speed to the doorway; whilst the half-awakened slumberers sank back again into deep sleep. Peter, not noticing this, rushed through the opening, thinking the knights were following him to inflict some terrible punishment on him—perhaps that of death—for his presumptuous intrusion. It was but a few moments, and he reached the boulder which defended the entrance, and which was much more difficult to scale from that side. He was endeavouring to find projections to enable him to clamber up, when he heard a hollow sepulchral voice exclaim from the cave :—

> " Potter, Potter Thompson,
> If thou had'st either drawn
> The sword or blown the horn,
> Thoud'st been the luckiest man
> That ever yet was born."

With teeth chattering, hair on end, and a cold perspiration suffusing his forehead, he made a desperate effort, scrambled somehow or other over the stone, and running with fleet footstep, regardless of the rough roadway, gained the open air without any other damage than a few bruises and a terrible fright. He went home, and had to encounter a fearful scolding for remaining out so long and neglecting his work. He told his wife the tale of his adventures, but she only laughed it to scorn, saying, " You old fool! and so you have fallen asleep on the hill-side and want to persuade me that your dream was a reality. Its a pretty thing that you should leave your wheel and go mooning about in this way, leaving your faithful wife to suffer the effects of your idleness."

Many a time since then did Peter seek for the ravine but could never find it; but it is confidently assumed that Arthur and his knights are still slumbering under the Castle hill.

The Doomed City.

THROUGH the valley of Wensleydale, in the North Riding of Yorkshire, flows the river Yore or Ure, passing onward to Boroughbridge, below which town it receives an insignificant affluent—the Ouse—when it assumes that name, under which appellation it washes the walls of York, and proceeds hence to unite with the Trent in forming the estuary of the Humber; but although it loses its name of Yore before reaching York, the capital city of the county is indebted to it for the name it bears. The river in passing through Wensleydale reflects on its surface some of the most romantic and charming landscape scenery of Yorkshire, and that is saying a great deal, for no other county can equal it in the variety, loveliness, and wild grandeur of its natural features.

"In this district, Wensleydale, otherwise Yorevale or Yorevalle," says Barker, "a variety

of scenery exists, unsurpassed in beauty by any
in England.   Mountains clothed at their summits
with purple heather, interspersed with huge
crags, and at their bases with luxuriant herbage,
bound the view on either hand.   Down the
valley's centre flows the winding Yore, one of the
most serpentine rivers our island boasts—now
boiling and foaming, in a narrow channel, over
sheets of limestone—now forming cascades only
equalled by the cataracts of the Nile—and anon
spreading out into a broad, smooth stream, as
calm and placid as a lowland lake.   On the banks
lie rich pastures, occasionally relieved, at the
eastern extremity of the valley, by cornfields.
There are several smaller dales branching out of
Wensleydale—of which they may, indeed, be
accounted part.   Of these the principal are
Bishopdale and Raydale, or Roedale—the valley
of the Roe—which last contains Lake Semerwater, a sheet of water covering a hundred and
five acres, and about forty-five feet deep.
Besides this lake, the natural objects of interest
in the district best known are Aysgarth Force,
Hardraw-scaur, Mill Gill, and Leyburn Shall—
the last a lofty natural terrace from which the
eye may range from the Cleveland Hills at the

mouth of the Tees to those bordering upon Westmoreland."

The valley is exceedingly rich in historic memories and noble monuments of the architectural past—"castles and halls inseparably united with English story, and abbeys whose names, whilst our national records shall be written, must for ever remain on the scroll; with fortresses which have been the palaces and prisons of kings. Of these, Bolton Castle, the home of the Scropes, and one of the prisons of Mary, Queen of Scots, and Middleham Castle, where dwelt the great Nevill, the king-maker, and the frequent and favourite residence of the Duke of Gloucester, afterwards King Richard III., and the venerable remains of Yorevale, or Jervaux, and of Coverham Abbeys, are alone sufficient to immortalise a district of country.

In former times the dale was covered by a dense forest, the home of countless herds of deer, wild boars, wolves, and other wild animals. There were no roads, but glades and trackways, intricate and winding, very difficult and puzzling to traverse, so that travellers often became benighted, without being able to find other shelter than that afforded by trees and bushes.

B

At the village of Bainbridge there is still
preserved the " forest horn," which was blown
every night at ten o'clock from Holyrood to
Shrovetide, to guide wanderers who had lost
their way to shelter and safety from the
prowling beasts of prey. A bell also was rung
at Chantry, and a gun fired at Camhouse with
the same object. In the first century of the
Christian era there existed in the valley of
Roedale a large and for that time splendid city,
inhabited by the Brigantian Celts. It nestled in
a deep hollow, surrounded by picturesque hills and
uplands, and was environed by the majestic trees
of the forest, where the Druids performed the
mystical rites and ceremonials of their religion.
The houses were built of mud and wattles, and
thatched with straw or reeds, and the city was a
mere assemblage of such private residences,
without any of the public buildings, such as
churches, chapels, town houses, assembly rooms,
baths, or literary institutions, such as now-a-days
appertain to every small market town; yet it
was spoken of as a " magnificent city," and such
it perhaps might be as compared with other and
smaller towns and villages.

It was about the time when Flavius Vespasian

annexed Britain to the Roman Empire, and the Brigantes had been partially subdued by Octavius Scapula, the Roman Governor of Britain, but before York had become Eboracum —the Altera Roma of Britain—and the influence of the conquerors of the world had not penetrated to this remote and secluded spot in the forest of Wensleydale, so that the people of the city still retained their old religion, customs, and habits of life ; still stained their bodies with woad, clothed themselves with the skins of animals, and still fabricated their weapons and implements of bronze.   Joseph of Arimathea had planted the cross on Glastonbury Hill, but the people of this city had never even heard of the new religion that had sprung up in Judea, and went on sacrificing human beings to their bloodthirsty god, cutting the sacred mistletoe from the oaks of their forest, and drawing the beaver from the water, emblematic of the salvation of Noah and his family at the deluge, of which they had a dim tradition.

The angels of heaven took great interest in the efforts of the apostles who, in obedience to their Master's command, went forth from Judea to preach the gospel of glad tidings and the doctrine of the cross to all mankind, and had especially noted the erection of the Christian standard on Glastonbury Hill, in the barbarous and benighted island of the Atlantic. One of the heavenly host, indeed, became so much interested in the conversion of the natives of this isle—which he foresaw would, in the distant centuries, become a great centre of evangelical truth, and, by means of missionaries, the foremost promulgator of religious light to other benighted peoples of the earth—that he determined to descend thither, and, under the guise of a human form, go about amongst the people, and in some measure prepare them for the reception of the teachings of the companions of St. Joseph.

Midwinter had come, the period when the sun seemed to the Britons to be farthest away from the earth, and when, according to the experience of the past, he would commence his return with his vivifying rays; and the Druids were holding joyous ceremonial in celebration of this annually recurring event. The sun was viewed as a superhuman beneficent being who journeyed across the heavens daily to dispense heat and life, and to cause the fruits and flowers and cereals to bloom and fructify, and give forth food for men and animals, who in summer approached near to the earth, and in winter retired to a distance from it—for what end or purpose they knew not. Nevertheless they deemed it wise to propitiate him by two great ceremonials of worship—the one at midsummer, attended by blazing "Baal-fires" on the hills (a custom which still survives in some parts of Yorkshire, where, on Midsummer-eve, "beal-fires" are lighted), a festival of rejoicing and thanksgiving for the ripening crops and fruits; the other at midwinter, which partook more of the character of a supplicating worship, imploring him, now that he was far distant, not to withdraw himself entirely from the earth, but return as he had been wont to do, and again cheer the world with his beams of brightness and warmth. On the occasion of this particular festival, the weather was stormy and cold; the pools were frozen over, and the ground covered with snow, whilst a chilling sleet, driven by a biting north-eastern wind, beat upon those who were exposed to its influence in the open air. The festival was proceeding in a cleared space of the forest circled round by lofty trees, which was the open-air natural temple of the Druids; its walls built by the hand of their god, and its

dome-like roof the floor of the habitation where
he dwelt. Whilst the Druids were engaged in
offering up prayers, the bards in singing anthems
of praise, and the vates investigating the entrails
of slain animals, to read therein forecasts of the
future and the will of the gods, especially of the
Sun God, in whose honour the festival was held,
the venerable figure of an aged man might be
seen descending the hill and approaching the
city. He seemed to be bowed down with the
infirmities of age, and to breast with difficulty
the forcible rushing of the wind. His white
flowing beard, which reached almost to his waist,
was glittering with incrustations of ice; and his
legs trembled as he came along, leaning on his
staff, with feeble and uncertain footsteps. He
was clad in a long gabardine, which he wrapped
tightly round him, to protect his frame as much
as possible from the inclemency of the weather;
his head was covered by a hat with broad
flapping brim; and his feet were sandalled, to
shield them from the roughness of the road.

He came amongst the cottages and passed
from door to door, asking for shelter and food,
but everywhere was repulsed, and at times with
contumely and opprobrious epithets. No one

would take him in beneath their roof; no one
had charity enough to give him a crust or a cup
of metheglin, and onward he went until he came
to the spot where the festival was progressing
under the direction of the Arch-Druid, a man of
extreme age, but of commanding stature and
majestic port.

The appearance of the angel (for he it was, in
the guise of infirm and poverty-stricken
humanity) caused some sensation, chiefly in
consequence of his peculiar and outlandish dress,
and all eyes were directed upon him as he walked
boldly and unhesitatingly, but with halting step,
to the centre of the circle where the hierarchs
were grouped.

The angel, addressing himself to the Arch-
Druid, inquired, " Whom is it that you worship
in this fashion ? "

" Who are you," replied the Druid, " that you
know not that our midwinter festival is in honour
of the great and gloriously shining God, who
reveals himself to us in his daily march across the
sky ? "

" Then you worship the creature instead of the
creator ? "

" How the creature ? He whom we worship

was never created, but has existed from all eternity."

" Alas! blind mortals, you labour under a Satanic delusion. Know that what you, in your ignorance, worship is but an atom in the great and resplendent universe of worlds and suns, called into existence by the fiat of Him whom I serve, who alone is self-existent, immortal, and the Creator of all men and all things."

" You speak in parables, stranger, and in an impious strain. Mean you to say that the god-sun is not great and powerful, he who causes the herbage to grow and the trees to give forth fruit? Can he do this if he be not a god?"

" He is merely the instrument of the one Almighty God, whose Son, on the anniversary of this day, became incarnate on earth, and died on the cross in a land far distant from this, that man might not be subjected to the penalty for dis-obedience to His laws, thus dying in his stead, to satisfy the ends of justice."

" And you say that he, a mere man, who died in the distant land you speak of, was the son of one who created the sun?"

" Most certainly."

"Then I must say that you speak rank blasphemy."

And the priests and other officials re-echoed the shout, "Blasphemy! blasphemy!" and the people around took it up, and the cry of "Blasphemy!" rose up from a thousand tongues.

"Slay him! stone him!" was then cried by the excited people, and they began to take up stones and hurl them at the old man, who, shaking the snow of the city from his sandals, and saying "Woe be unto you," passed through the surrounding crowd, and disappeared amongst the forest trees.

The dusky shades of evening, or rather afternoon, were drawing in as the angel passed through the wood; and as, in his incarnate form, he was subject to all the sufferings and discomforts humanity is liable to, he feared that he would have to pass the night, with all its inclemency of weather, with no other shelter than that afforded by a tree trunk or the branches of a bramble bush, but after wandering some time he came upon a cleared space, where he found some sheep huddling together on the lee side of a rising ground, and judging that where sheep were men would not be far distant, he passed up

the hillside and gladly hailed a gleam of light
issuing from a cottage window.   He approached
and knocked at the door, which was opened by a
comely, middle-aged dame, whilst, by the fire of
peat, sat a man whom he presumed to be her
husband, occupied in eating his evening meal,
with a shepherd dog by his side, eagerly looking
out for the bones and chance pieces of meat
which his master might think proper to throw
him.

"Good dame," said he to the woman, "have
you charity enough to give me shelter from the
storm, a crust of bread to allay the cravings of
hunger, and permission to imbibe warmth from
your fire into my aged and frozen limbs?"

"Yes, that indeed we have, venerable father,"
replied she.   "Come in and seat you by the fire,
and we will see what the cottage can supply in
the way of victuals."

He stepped in, and was welcomed with equal
kindness by the husband, who placed for him a
seat near the fire, took off his coat, which he
suspended before the fire to dry, and gave him a
sheepskin to throw over his shoulders; whilst
the dame bustled about in the way of cooking
some slices of mutton and bringing out some of

her best bread, with a wooden drinking vessel
filled with home-made barley liquor, not unlike
the ale of after days.

He was then invited to seat himself at the
table, a board resting on two trestles, and ate
heartily of the viands before him. After the
meal, and when he was thoroughly warmed and
made comfortable, he entered into conversation
with the worthy couple, and ascertained that the
man was a shepherd, and made a fairly comfortable living out of his small flock of sheep, which
supplied him and his wife with raiment and flesh
meat for food, besides a small surplus for barter
to procure other necessaries. He told them that
he was a wanderer on the face of the earth, not a
Briton, but allied to people who lived in the far
east near the sun rising, and that he had come
hither to tell the Britons of the true God, and
that they whom they worshipped were not gods
at all; to all which they listened with wonder-
ment and awe, but displayed none of the bigotry
and hostility to adverse faiths which had been so
practically shown in the city. With eloquent
tongue he explained to them the mysteries of the
Christian religion, but they comprehended him
not, such matters being entirely beyond the

capacities of their understandings. Nevertheless they were much interested in some of the narratives, such as the nativity and the visit of the Magi ; the miraculous cures of the sick ; the crucifixion, the resurrection, and the ascension, all which were told with great graphic power, and listened to with rapt ears ; and they sat on late into the night in this converse, and then a bed of several layers of straw was made for the stranger in a warm corner of the cottage, and a couple of sheep skins given him for coverlets.

The following morning broke bright and cheerful, a complete contrast to the preceding day. The sun came out with a radiance as brilliant as it was possible for a midwinter sun to do, and lighted up the hills, on which the snow crystals glistened, and the roofs of the houses in the valley below, with a splendour seldom beheld at that period of the year, and the people of the city hailed the sight as a response to their festival prayers, that the God of Day would still continue to shower his blessings upon them, and bring forth their crops and fruits in due course. The guest at the shepherd's cottage, wearied with his wanderings and the buffeting of the storm, slept long after the sun had risen ; but his hosts had been up betimes, the shepherd having gone to look after his sheep, and his wife to prepare a warm breakfast for him on his return. When this was ready, and the shepherd had come home, their guest was awakened, and partook with them of their meal of sheep's flesh, brown bread, and ewe's milk. He had performed certain devotions on rising, such as his entertainers understood not, but which they assumed to be acts of adoration and thanksgiving to his God.

Resuming his cloak, now thoroughly dried, his flapped hat, and his long walking staff, he went out to pursue his journey. With his hosts he stood on the elevated ground on which the cottage was situated, and looked down upon the city in the valley below, from which there rose up the busy hum of voices of men going about their vocations for the day, with them the first of their new-born year.

The stranger looked down upon the city for some moments in silence; then stretching forth his arms towards it, he exclaimed, " Oh city! thou art fair to look upon, but thou art the habitation of hard, unfeeling, and uncharitable men, who regard themselves alone, and neither respect age nor sympathise with poverty and infirmity! Thou art the abode of those who worship false gods, and shut their ears to, nay, more, maltreat those who would point out their errors and lead them into the path of truth; therefore, oh city! it is fitting that thou shouldst cease to cumber the earth; that thou shouldst be swept away as were Sodom and Gomorrah. As for you," he added, turning to the shepherd and his wife, "you took the stranger in under your roof, sheltered him from the storm, fed him when ahungered, and comforted him as far as your means permitted. For this accept my thanks and benison, and know that my benison is worth the acceptance, for I am not what I seem—a frail mortal—but one of those who stand round the throne of the God I told you of last evening, which is in the midst of the stars of the firmament. May your flocks increase, and your crops never fail; may you live to advanced age, and see your children and children's children grow up around you, wealthy in this world's wealth, honoured, and respected." Turning again towards the city, and again stretching forth his arms over it, the mysterious stranger cried out in a voice that might be heard in the streets below :—

"Semerwater, rise; Semerwater, sink;
  And swallow all the town, save this lile
  House, where they gave me meat and drink."

Immediately a loud noise was heard, as of the bursting up of a hundred fountains from the earth, and the water rushed upward from every part of the city like the vomiting of volcanoes; the inhabitants cried out with terror-fraught shouts, and attempted to escape up the hills, but were swept back by the surging flood, which waved and dashed like the waves of the tempestuous sea. Higher and higher rose the water; overwhelmed the houses and advanced up the sides of the hill, engulfing everything and destroying every vestige of life, and eventually it settled down into the vast lake as it may now be seen.

It may be thought that this was a cruel act of revenge on the part of the angel, but we have the authority of Milton, that the angelic mind was susceptible of the human weakness of ambition; why, therefore, should it not be actuated by that other human passion of revenge?

The shepherd and his wife gazed on the spectacle of the destruction of the city with awe-

stricken countenances, when another spectacle
filled them with equal amazement.   They turned
their eyes upon their guest, who still stood by
them, but who was undergoing a wonderful
transformation.   From an aged and infirm man
he was becoming youthful in appearance, of noble
figure, with lineaments of celestial beauty, and an
aureola of golden light flashing round his head.
His tattered and way-worn garments seemed to
be melting into thin air and passing away, and in
their place appeared a long white robe, as if
woven of the snow crystals of the surrounding
hills; whilst from his shoulders there streamed
forth a pair of pinions, which he now expanded,
and waving an adieu to his late entertainers, he
rose up into the air, and in a few minutes had
passed beyond their sight.

The shepherd's flocks soon began to multiply
wonderfully, and he speedily became one of the
richest men of the countryside.   His sons grew
up and prospered as their father had, and their
descendants flourished for many generations in
their several branches as some of the most
important and wealthy families of the district.
The old man and his wife abandoned the old
Druidical religion, and prayed to the unknown

God of whom their guest spoke on the memorable evening preceding the destruction of the city; and when the Apostles of Christianity came hither, were among the first converts. There may be sceptics who may doubt the truth of this legend, but there the Lake of Semerwater still remains, and what can be a more convincing proof of its truth, as old Willet was wont to say, when pointing to the block of wood at the door of his inn at Chigwell, as a triumphant proof of the truth of the story he had been narrating. The rustics of the neighbourhood also assert that they have seen, fathoms deep in the lake, the chimneys and church spires of the engulfed city; but as there were neither churches nor chimneys when that city was in existence, we are inclined to believe that this is an optical delusion.

The "Worm" of Nunnington.

 CHARMING pastoral scene might have been witnessed in the picturesque valley of Ryedale, northward of Malton, and not far distant from the spot where, in after ages, sprung up the towers of Byland Abbey, one fair midsummer eve in the earlier half of the sixth century—a scene that would have gladdened the heart of a painter, and made him eager to transfer it to canvas, to display it on the walls of the next Royal Academy Exhibition, had painters and Royal Academy Exhibitions been then in vogue. It was in a village near the banks of the Rye—the precursor of what is now called Nunnington; what was its Celtic name we are informed not, but it was a Celtic village, and inhabited by Celtic people, who had been Christianised, and taught the usages and habits of civilized life during the supremacy of the Romans in the island, who had now departed to defend the capital of the world

against the incursions of the hordes of barbarians who were thundering at its gates, leaving the Britons, enervated by civilisation and its attendant luxuries, a prey to the Picts and Scots and the Teutonic pirates who infested the surrounding seas.

It was an age of chivalry and romance; the half real, half mythical Arthur ruled over the land, and made head against the Scots and the Teutons, defeating both in several battles. He instituted the chivalric Order of Knights of the Round Table—whose members were patterns of valour and exemplars in religion, and who went forth as knights-errant to correct abuses, protect the fairer and weaker sex, chastise oppressors, release those who were under spells of enchantment, and do battle with giants, ogres, malicious dwarfs, and enchanters, also with dragons, hippogriffs, wyverns, serpents, and other similarly obnoxious creatures. Who hath not read of their marvellous adventures and valorous exploits in the quest of the Sang-real, the histories of Sir Launcelot and Sir Tristram, La Morte d'Arthur, and the Idylls of the King? Witches and warlocks, sorcerers and ogres, tyrants and oppressors, then abounded in the

land, and beauteous damsels, the victims of their
cruelty and lust, so that there was plenty of
work, to say nothing of the reptiles of the forests,
for the entire army of valiant knights who went
forth from Caerleon on the Usk in quest of
adventures, inspired by the approving smile of
Queen Guinevere and of the fair ladies in whose
honour they placed lance in rest, and whose
supremacy of beauty they vowed to maintain in
many a joust and tournament.

The village lay in a spot where nature had
spread out some of her loveliest features of valley,
upland, and meandering river of silvery sheen
running through the midst; whilst trees of
luxuriant foliage, in groups and thickets of forest
land, enshrined the whole as a fitting frame-
work for the sylvan picture. Farmsteads were
scattered about, and a cluster of humbler
cottages, the habitations of the serf class of farm
labourers constituted the village.

As we have seen, it was Midsummer Eve, a
day of festival and rejoicing which had been
observed from time immemorial, for now the sun
approached the nearest to the zenith with its
fructifying beams, and in celebration of the event
a huge bonfire had been built up on an eminence

outside the village ; whilst around it, hand in
hand, danced the youths and maidens with much
glee and merriment, with boisterous mirth, and
many a joke and song, and moreover with no
lack of flirtation between the lads and lasses, who
footed it merrily, and became more and more
vigorous in the dances as the flames mounted
higher and higher. Although they knew it not,
this village carnival was a survival of the
paganism of the past, when the remote ancestors
of the existing generation worshipped Baal, the
great Sun God. It had come down through
centuries of homage to the creature instead of
the Creator, and having been regarded as a great
holiday, did not suffer extinction at the advent of
Christianity, but was permitted to be retained in
that capacity, without any reference to religious
ceremonial, which in course of time was entirely
forgotten. And it is a remarkable instance of
the vitality of ancient customs to observe that in
some parts of Yorkshire, in Holderness to wit,
"Beal fires" are lighted on Midsummer Eve,
even to the present day.

The elders of the village were seated about in
groups on the turf, watching the upblazing of the
fire, casting approving smiles on the joyous

gambols and incipient match-making of their
progeny, and talking of their own juvenile days,
when they were equally happy partners in the
circling dance. The blue sky overhead was
cloudless, and in the western horizon the setting
sun shot forth beams of golden light; and all
was hilarity and happiness. A queen of the
festival had been chosen—the most beautiful
maiden of the village, a sweet girl of eighteen,
with brilliant complexion, melting blue eyes, and
flowing curls of flaxen hue. A platform of
boughs had been improvised upon which to carry
her on the shoulders of a half-dozen young
bachelors back to the village with songs of
triumph, and the procession had just been
arranged, when a loud hissing sound was heard
to issue from the neighbouring forest, a sound
which in these days would have been attributed
to a passing railway train; but which then
sounded strange and unearthly, and spread
consternation among the merrymakers, who
turned and looked with panic-stricken countenances in the direction from whence the sound
came.

The first impulse of the crowd was to fly to
their homes, from the unknown object of dread,

but curiosity prompted a counter-impulse, a
desire to see what gave rise to the fear-inspiring
sound. Nor had they long to wait, for a few
minutes after a monstrous reptile, with the body
of a serpent and the head of a dragon, its mouth
seeming, to their excited imaginations, to breathe
out flame, issued from the wood and came across
the open space with fearful but graceful undula-
tions towards the terrified villagers. The air
appeared to become charged, too, with a pestiferous influence, issuing from the nostrils of the
monster, which increased in intensity the nearer
it came. With shrieks and wild cries, those who
had been dancing so merrily but a few minutes
before took to their heels to find refuge in their
cottages, exclaiming, "Oh, that Sir Peter Loschi
were here to deliver us from the monster!" All
reached their habitations and barred their doors :
all save one, the beautiful young queen of the
festival, the pride of the village—the beloved of
every one—who, fascinated like a bird by the eyes
of the reptile, had stood gazing upon it so long
that she was quite in the rear of the fugitives,
and was overtaken by the serpent, who immediately coiled the foremost part of its body round
her, and in this fashion carried her back into the

forest. As she did not reappear, it was concluded that she had been devoured; and day after day one young damsel after another disappeared after going to the spring for water, or on other open-air errands, all of whom, it was doubted not, had furnished meals for the monster. Indeed, at times he was seen carrying them off as he had done the poor little queen, until at length the village seemed to be becoming depopulated of its maidenhood. The men at times went armed with bludgeons to attack the serpent in his cave on the hill side, but were ever driven back by the poisonous exhalations of the animal's breath, which seemed to render them faint and powerless; and two or three of the bolder spirits who approached the nearest to the den died under its influence. And the people continued to cry, " Oh, Sir Peter Loschi, why do you tarry ?"—for in him lay all their hope of deliverance.

This Sir Peter Loschi, whose aid was so frequently and fervently invoked, was the owner of a castle and certain broad acres in the vicinity. He was a Celt of unadulterated blood, although his name has nothing Celtic about it. Single names were then only used, with the exception of an addition of some personal characteristic or locality, for distinction sake when there were two persons bearing the same, and we may suppose that the two names of Peter and Loschi originally formed one word, which has become altered and corrupted in passing from generation to generation, in a similar manner to that of George Zavier, which became transmuted through Georgy Zavier, etc., to eventually Corky Shaver. Be that as it may, he was the last male of a long line of ancient British knights and warriors, and was himself not inferior to any of his ancestors in military skill and almost reckless daring, having fought with distinction against the wild hordes of Picts and Scots, who came down from their desolate northern mountains to make raids on the more fertile lands of the Britons south of the Border, and against the piratical Saxons and Angles who were endeavouring to get a foothold on the island. He was one of King Arthur's Knights of the Round Table, and was often at the Court of Queen Guinevere at Caerleon, consorting with his brother knights in the mutual recital of their adventures, in friendly tilting matches, and in dallying with the fair ladies of the Court, one of whom he had chosen as the mistress of his

heart, and whose favour he wore in front of his
helmet at many a passage of arms in the court-
yard of a castle or in the field of a tournament.
Occasionally he went forth for periods of six or
twelve months as a knight-errant, for the purpose
of redressing wrongs, slaying enchanters, etc.,
and was known as the Knight of the Sable
Plume, from that ornamental appendage of his
casque. The cognisance that he bore on his
shield was a chevron arg. between three plumes
sable, on ground or; and many a doughty deed
had he performed, young as he still was, under
this cognisance.

He did not spend much time at his ancestral
home in Ryedale, being so much occupied at
Court and in the quest of adventures as a knight-
errant, only going there occasionally to regulate
matters relating to his household and estates,
look after his vassals and retainers, and make
arrangements for the well-being of the villagers.
He had now been absent about three years,
having, at the instance of his ladye-love at
Caerleon, donned his armour, taken his lance in
hand, and gone for that space of time to protect
the impotent, redress the injured and oppressed,
and slay giants and sorcerers, as a test of his

valour, at the end of which said period, if he had acquitted himself as a preux-chevalier, she might possibly consent to become the mistress of Ryedale Castle. The period was now drawing to a close, and he had performed many a valorous deed; he had slain a gigantic Saxon in single combat; he had recovered the standard of King Arthur from some half-dozen Picts, who had seized it after killing the bearer of it; he had rescued a damsel from the hands of an enchanter; another from the fangs and claws of a lion, and a third from a giant who was dragging her along by the hair of her head; he had killed a dragon, a griffin, and a hippogriff, had done many another wondrous and valorous deed, and was now going back to Caerleon to claim the hand of the lady at whose behest he had performed all these marvellous achievements, little dreaming all the time that his own people in Ryedale were in sore need of his stalwart arm and trusty sword.

As the knight had been northward, it was necessary to pass through what is now Yorkshire on his way to Caerleon, and he deemed it expedient to call at his Ryedale Castle to see how matters had been going on there during his long absence.

It was about a month after the first appearance
of the "worm," when the villagers were
beginning to experience the truth of the saying
that "hope deferred maketh the heart sick,"
having lost many members of their community
through the propensity of the serpent for human
flesh, and no Sir Peter coming to deliver them
from the ravages of the monster, when the figure
of a horseman, with a nodding black plume, was
seen "pricking o'er the plain," who was immediately recognised as the veritable Sir Peter
Loschi, which gave rise to an exhilarating shout
of welcome from the villagers, who cried, "Now
shall we be delivered from the ravenous worm."
Sir Peter rode on to his castle, where the first
being to welcome him was a favourite mastiff,
who came gambolling about him with the most
affectionate demonstrations of rejoicing at seeing
his master once more. The following morning a
deputation of the villagers waited upon him,
explained their troubles in respect to the worm,
and prayed for his assistance in ridding them of
the monster. He inquired into the particulars,
and having been accustomed in his travels to
several encounters with noxious animals of this
character, he readily understood what he would

have to deal with, and promised his aid, but added that as some preparations would be necessary, the enemy being of an exceptional description, he would not be able to undertake it within a month, and that they must endure it the best they could in the interval.

Sir Peter got a sight of the serpent, and a formidable monster he appeared to be, more terrible than any he had previously met with; and he saw that it behoved him to make special provision for the combat. He pondered the matter over for a few days, and then mounted his steed and rode to Sheffield, where he employed certain cunning artificers to make him a complete suit of armour studded with razor blades. Although razors are alluded to by Homer, and have been used by the Chinese for unknown centuries, it is doubtful whether they were a staple manufacture on the banks of the Sheaf and the Rivelin in the sixth century. It is true that Chaucer speaks of a "Sheffield whittle," but this was eight centuries afterwards, and it is equally to be doubted whether Sheffield, even as a village, existed at that time; but anachronisms are of small moment in legends, and we are required to accept it as a fact, that the knight had his novel suit of armour fabricated in the valley of the Sheaf.

When it was completed, he returned with it to Ryedale, and gladly was he welcomed by the villagers, as the serpent had been committing more ravages amongst the population. He had a sword, a Damascus blade of wonderful keenness, which possessed certain magical properties, similar to those of King Arthur's famous Excaliber; and one morning, after donning his armour, he took the sword in his hand and went forth to the combat. His dog accompanied him, and it was with difficulty that he was prevented from leaping up in caressing gambols against the sharp razor blades.

The serpent had its den in the side of a wooded eminence near East Newton, by Stonegrave, which has since then gone by the name of Loschy Hill, in memory of the great fight between the Knight and the Dragon. Sir Peter, who was on foot, strode along boldly towards the hill, followed by his dog, which seemed to be perfectly aware that some exciting sport was before them, as he rushed about hither and thither, sniffing the air, as if his keen scent gave him intimation that game of an unusual character was not far off, and he barked and growled, as if in defiance of the foe; whilst the villagers stood afar off, with eager countenances, to watch the progress of the combat. As the knight came nearer, he became aware of a pestiferous odour that seemed to contaminate the air; and the dog scented and sniffed, and gave vent to more prolonged growlings and louder barking, and seemed to tremble with excitement in anticipation of the coming fray.

The serpent had not yet breakfasted, and seeing the man and dog approach, darted from his den and made for the dog, with which he thought to stay his appetite as a first mouthful, but the dog was too nimble and eluded his attack, leaping upon one of the curves of its body and biting it with mad excitement; whilst the knight struck it a blow with his sword which almost cut off its head, but the wound healed up instantly, and the serpent coiled itself round his body, in order to crush the life out of him, and then devour him at its leisure. It had not, in doing so, taken into account the razor blades, which cut its body in a multitude of gashes, and caused the blood to stream down on the earth; but this was not of much consequence, as it immediately uncoiled and

rolled itself on the earth, when all the wounds
closed up. Foiled in this attack, the monster
then began to vomit out a poisonous vapour, so
horrible and overcoming that the knight seemed
ready to sink under its influence, but rallying his
energies, he aimed a blow which cut the serpent
in two, but the severed parts joined again immediately. All this time the monster was hissing
in a fearful manner, and breathing out poison,
and the knight began to fear he must succumb
and become its prey; but determined not to give
in so long as he could continue the fight, he
aimed another blow with his sword and severed a
portion of the tail end, although feeling persuaded
that it would become reunited as before; but his
dog, evidently a sagacious animal, having witnessed the former reunion, seized it in its teeth
and ran off with it to a neighbouring hill, then
returned and carried away other portions as they
were cut off successively. The serpent writhed
with pain, but afraid, or seeing the uselessness of
attacking the razor-armed man, made many
attempts to seize the dog, but in vain, as he was
too agile to be caught; therefore he depended
more on the venom of his breath at this juncture,
which he continued to pour forth, and which he

knew must eventually overpower his enemy.
The dog had returned from his third or fourth
journey and came up to his master, wagging his
tail in seeming congratulation of the cleverness
with which they were gradually accomplishing
the destruction of the foe, when the serpent made
a spring upon him, but at the same instant the
knight's magic sword descended upon his neck
and severed the head from the body, which the
dog at once seized and carried off to a distance,
placing it on a hill near where Nunnington
Church now stands.

The monster was now dead which had caused
so much terror and desolation, and the villagers
shouted with joy as they saw the head carried
past by the dog. Meanwhile the knight stood by
the remaining portion of the body as it lay prone
on the earth, quivering with the remains of its
vitality. He was exhausted with his exertions,
but more by the poisonous exhalation which the
body still gave forth, but in rapidly diminishing
volume. He was recovering from its effects and
was waiting awhile to gain sufficient energy to
leave the scene of his triumph, when the dog
returned, but apparently in a very languid
condition; still, however, evincing marks of

D

satisfaction and pleasure at the conquest he and his master had achieved. The knight stooped down to pat caressingly his faithful companion, who, in return, reached up and licked his face. Unfortunately, in carrying away the head, the seat of the venom, the dog had imbibed the poison, and in licking his master's face had imparted the virus to him, and a few minutes were sufficient to produce its fatal effects, the knight and his dog falling to the earth together, and when the villagers came up they found both dead.

Although the villagers were rejoiced at the death of the serpent, their lamentations were equally great over the fate of the knight, who had sacrificed his life for their deliverance; and for many a month and year did they cherish his memory and mourn his death.

In Nunnington Church there is a monument of a knight, a recumbent effigy, with a dog crouching at his feet; and this, tradition says, is the tomb of the valorous Sir Peter Loschi and his equally valorous dog, who were buried together, and the monument erected in grateful memory of their achievement.

The Devil's Arrows.

ONE of the most interesting localities in broad Yorkshire, rich in historic lore and fruitful in legend, is that which comprehends within its limits the twin towns of Aldborough and Boroughbridge, on the river Ure. Their history extends back to the Celtic and Roman times, when Aldborough or Iseur, the Isurium of the Romans, was the capital of the Brigantian Celts, and near by ran northward from York a great Roman road, which crossed the Ure by a ford, which was supplanted after the Conquest by a wooden bridge, which gave rise to a great convergence of roads at this point, and the growth of a town, which obtained the name of Boroughbridge, i.e., the borough by the bridge.

This spot, says Dr. Stukeley, was in the British time "the scene of the great Panegyre of the Druids, the midsummer meeting of all the country round, to celebrate the great quarterly sacrifice, accompanied with sports, games, races, and all kinds of exercises, with universal festivity. This was like the Olympian and Nemean meetings and games among the Grecians."

Between the two towns there stands protruding from the earth three rough-hewn and weather-worn obelisks of rag-stone or mill-stone grit, which could not have been brought from a distance of less than seven miles, and gave rise to a sense of wonder how such stupendous masses could have been brought hither and placed upright in position by the Celts with their utter lack of mechanical appliances. The northernmost rises eighteen feet, the southernmost twenty-two and a half feet, and the centre one also twenty-two and a half feet above the ground, and from an excavation made under the latter, it was found to have an entire length of thirty feet six inches. The estimated weight of the northernmost is thirty-six tons, and of the other two thirty tons each. Originally there were four stones, which were seen by Leland in Henry VIII.'s time; but one of them fell or was removed for the sake of the materials—useful for road repairing—in the seventeenth century. Camden imagined them to be factitious compositions of sand, lime, and small pebbles cemented together; but there is no doubt they were quarried at Plumpton, the rock there corresponding exactly with their grit. The Romans made use of them as metæ, the turning point in their chariot races. There have been varying and differing conjectures by antiquaries as to their origin and purpose, but all agree as to their remote antiquity, dating back certainly 1800 years, the most probable conjecture as to their purpose being that they were connected in some way with Druidical worship. They go by the name of "The Devil's Arrows," and tradition gives an account of their origin altogether different from antiquarian conjectures, and much more in accordance with their popular designation. Thus runs the legend :-

It was soon after the Crucifixion that certain Apostles of the Cross, headed by Joseph of Arimathea, found their way from Palestine to the remote and benighted isle of Britain, in obedience to the Divine command to go forth and preach the Gospel to every creature. After their disembarkation they proceeded inland until they came to Glastonbury; and ascending the hill there, Joseph struck his walking staff in the earth and proclaimed that there should be established the first Christian church of Britain, and in confirmation thereof his staff miraculously took root, put forth branches, and although it was midwinter—Christmas day—budded and blossomed into a rose, as its successors here continued to do on every successive Christmas Day. The Apostles preached to the barbarian people, made some converts, and erected a temporary wooden church for the performance of divine service, which was the precursor of the magnificent Abbey that afterwards rose on the site, and flourished in great prosperity until its extinction under the sacrilegious hand of Henry the Eighth.

When the new faith had taken root at Glastonbury, the Apostles divided themselves into bands of two or three, and departed north, south, east, and west, to proclaim the glad tidings in other parts of the island. One of these bands, going northwards, preached to the Cornabii and the Coritani of Mid-Britain, and then passed onward to the Brigantes, the greatest and most warlike of the kingdoms of Britain. They travelled on foot, staff in hand, and subsisted on the charity of the people; but

had often to endure great hardships, having often
to pass through scantily peopled districts, where
wild fruits were their only food, the water of the
wayside brooks their drink, and their sleeping
couches the heather of the moor or the turf
under the canopy of a forest tree. But all these
discomforts they endured with cheerfulness,
besides perils from wolves, wild boars, and other
denizens of the woodlands, feeling assured that
their Master would reward them a thousand-fold
for their sufferings in His service.

On entering the Brigantian kingdom they
learned that the capital city was Iseur, some considerable distance northward, and thither they
bent their way in the hope of enlightening the
King in spiritual matters as a means of facilitating
the conversion of his people. With wearied steps
they passed from village to village, through
forests and swamps, and over black moorlands,
fording the rivers where practicable, or where
they were too deep for so doing going along the
bank until they met with a fisherman or villager
to ferry them across in his coracle; and in due
course, after many days of toilsome journeying,
came to the city of Iseur.

The city stood in a forest clearing, surrounded

by a stockade of felled trees, with an entrenchment for protection against enemies, and for the security of their flocks and herds against the attacks of wild beasts. In the centre stood the King's Palace, a tolerably spacious edifice built of unhewn blocks of stone, placed in cyclopean fashion without mortar; and scattered around were the mud-built and straw-thatched dwellings of the people. There was no temple of their deity, the gods of the Britons disdaining mortal-built places of worship. But adjacent was a separate forest clearing, with a circling of huge forest oaks, on which grew the sacred mistletoe, which constituted a temple not built with hands; and in which was a pool of water, indispensable in the ceremonials of their religion, where the beaver abounded, and was used as an emblem of the flood, of which the Britons had a tradition; and here were constructed the wickerwork forms of gigantic human beings, which at certain seasons were filled with men, women, and children, and burnt to propitiate the wrath of their god.

They proceeded to the palace of the King and asked for an audience, which was granted them after some demur; the King feeling uncertain,

from the description his attendants gave of their
foreign aspect, outlandish dresses, and imperfect
utterance of the British language, whether they
might not be enemies, assassins, or sorcerers
come hither to take his life or subject him to
some other evil. He received them seated on a
sort of throne, clad in a white, coarsely woven
tunic of wool reaching half way down his thighs,
and leaving the lower limbs altogether uncovered,
and over his shoulders a wolf-skin mantle,
whilst he supported his dignity by holding in his
right hand a long bronze-headed spear, with a
richly-carved shaft. By his side sat his Queen,
and at his feet gambolled three or four children,
whilst around him stood representatives of the
Druidical hierarchy—the Druids proper or high
priests, the Eubates or soothsayers, and the
Bards who chanted anthems to the glory of
their god and recited odes in praise of the
warriors and great men of their race.

The King inquired of the strangers who they
were and what was their purpose in thus coming
to his court. The Apostles replied that they
were people of a far distant land, near the
sun-rising, and had come hither to show them
their errors in worshipping false gods, and point

out to them the true object of worship, the one
only God, the Maker of heaven and earth, and
the awarder of happiness or misery in the future
life beyond the grave. A murmur of dissatis-
faction arose at this announcement amongst the
Druids, who whispered amongst themselves that
it was fitting such blasphemers should be offered
up as sacrifices to their god.

"Truly," said the King, "you have come on a
strange errand ; we are firm believers in and
devout worshippers of the one Supreme God, as
you pretend to be. Do we not yearly offer up
on His altars hundreds of human victims to
propitiate His good-will ? What more would
you have ? We believe what you do, and a great
deal more, for we have a host of minor deities
whom we pay adoration to. Methinks you had
better return to your own country and not
trouble us with your hallucinations, so as to
cause a schism in the faith. We are content
with our own belief, which teaches us that when
we die the souls of those who have done justly
will pass gradually into a higher and higher
sphere, until at length, when perfectly purified, it
will become absorbed in the essence of the Deity,
or become an inferior god; whilst those of the

wicked will be transformed to the bodies of inferior and unclean animals, and eventually be annihilated."

The Apostles upon this explained briefly the principles of the Christian religion, the fall of man and his loss of the divine favour, his necessary condemnation to temporal and eternal death, and the redemptorial scheme, in which God himself, or rather his Son, who was identical with himself, suffered death on the cross, taking upon himself, in lieu of man, the threatened penalty.

"Is your God dead, then?" inquired the King; "or is it possible for God to die. If so, our faith is better than yours, for our God is immortal."

The Apostles then entered into an elaborate disquisition on the subleties of the necessity and nature of the Divine scheme for the salvation of the human race, but the reasonings were too abstruse for the King's comprehension, as, indeed, were they for the more cultured minds of the Druids; therefore the King declined any further discourse on the subject, adding that he was perfectly willing that they should be courteously treated and have fair play, as they had come so far with the intent, as it seemed to them, of doing him and his people a service; therefore he would appoint a day on which they should have a full and fair discussion with the Druids on the merits of the respective faiths, and in the meantime they should be hospitably entertained at his cost, and with this the audience terminated.

It happened that at this time the Father of Evil was prowling about Britain, with the object of thwarting the efforts of St. Joseph and his band of missionaries for the evangelisation of the land. He employed himself chiefly about Glastonbury and its neighbourhood, the primitive and central seat of British Christianity, and centuries elapsed before he relaxed his persistent attempt to eradicate the faith, hostile to himself, which had taken root there. Nine hundred years afterwards we find that he was a perpetual annoyance to the holy St. Dunstan in his Glastonbury cell, continually intruding upon him when engaged in his studies, and offering to him the most seductive temptations, until, on one occasion, he made his appearance before him when he was engaged on some blacksmith work, and commenced tempting him to sell his soul to him for unbounded wealth and the highest temporal distinction. The saint, however, was proof against his temptations, and resolved to free himself once for all from his importunities, took his red-hot tongs from the fire, and seized him by the nose. The devil roared out lustily with the pain, although one would fancy, from fire being his natural element, that it would not incommode him greatly; nevertheless, he prayed abjectly to be released from the tongs, but the saint would not release him until he promised to give him no further annoyance.

He had followed in the footsteps of the three Apostles on the northern mission, and was present, although invisible, at the interview with the King of the Brigantes; and when the conference between the Apostles and the Druids was arranged by the King, he determined upon presenting himself at the meeting in a more tangible and palpable form, to overthrow the arguments of the former by the power of his eloquence and logical force of reasoning, feeling exceedingly loth to run the risk of losing so cherished a section of his dominions, which would ensue in case the King should be convinced by the preaching and the powerful arguments of the Apostles.

The conference was appointed to come off on the slopes of the Hambleton Hills, at the foot of Roulston Crag and there, on the auspicious morning, might be seen a large assemblage gathered together, presenting a very animated and picturesque grouping. The King, as president of the assembly, took his seat on an improvised throne. He was clothed in the most splendid of his regal vestments, and held in his hand his bronze-headed spear, as an emblem of his Royal authority. On his right stood a group of Druids, clad in long white linen robes, with circlets of oak leaves round their heads, and on his left the three Christian Apostles, in their weather-stained Oriental garments, whilst scattered around, was a considerable number of Brigantian warriors, courtiers, agriculturists, and serfs more or less garmented in coarse woollen fabrics or skins of animals, or without clothing of any kind, but with painted or tattooed skins, on which were depicted figures of the sun, the moon, and sundry animals. The King opened the proceedings by stating the object of the meeting, and calling upon the Apostles to explain what they wished to inculcate, promising them a fair and candid hearing, and assuring them that if what they said appeared at all consonant with reason, it should have due consideration. In all respects the meeting was very similar to that which was convened nearly 600 years afterwards by Eadwine, King of Northumbria, for a discussion of the merits of Christianity, between St. Paulinus, the apostle of Rome, and Coiffi, the High Priest of Woden, which resulted in the second establishment of Christianity in the district, which constitutes the modern Yorkshire. Just as one of the Apostles was commencing to speak, a venerable Druid, with a beard reaching half-way down to his waist, and attired in the official long white robe, entered the assembly, and made his obeisance to the King, who inquired who he was and whither he had come. "I am the High Priest, oh King," he replied, "of the great and famous forest temple of Llyn yr a vane" (on the site of the modern Beverley). "A report came thither that certain strangers had come to the Court of Iseur from some distant land, to promulgate a foreign and damnable heresy; and I, as being well versed in the truths of our faith, and gifted with an eloquent tongue, have been deputed by my brethren to attend this conference, and aid, to the best of my ability, in discomfiting these foreign heretics, whose object is to uproot our holy religion and substitute a false theological creed."

"You are welcome!" said the King. "Take your place among your brother Druids on my right. Give heed to what the strangers have to say, and reply to their arguments as your reason and lengthened experience may dictate."

The stranger took the place indicated, and the King bade the Apostles tell what they had to say on the object of their mission, upon which the eldest looking of the three, stretching forth his arms as Raphael depicted Paul when preaching at Athens, commenced his harangue by giving an outline of the history of man as recorded in the Scriptures, his fall from innocence and perfection, by the seductions of the enemy of mankind, who for his rebellious ambition had been banished from heaven and cast down into hell, and who since then had been going to and fro in the earth tempting man to sin against his Maker, in which he had been so successful that God repented of having made man, and had caused all mankind to perish save one family, and then explained that afterwards, when the earth had again become populated, he compassionated man's fallen estate, and had sent his Son to take on himself the penalty due to man's transgression, that all, through him, might be placed in a state of salvation from that death eternal which they inherited from the transgression of their first ancestor; and wound up by imploring the King and all present to abandon their impotent and bloodthirsty gods, believe in the God of Mercy whom they proclaimed, and accept the salvation offered through the merits of Him who was crucified.

The Druid, who had come afar, then rose and craved permission to reply, which was granted, and he stood forth on a mass of rock, with a majestic presence and dignified air. He laughed to scorn the fables which they had listened to, which were only fit to delude the ears of silly old women, and could not be accepted for a moment by men endowed with the faculty of reasoning. "We are told," said he, "that man was made perfect, and was at the same time fallible; that God is immutable, and yet repented; that a creature, the work of His hands, has become His rival, and from what we hear has become even more potent than his Maker; has set up a rival kingdom, and is able to wrest from the hands of

E

God three-fourths of the beings whom He creates, a God who is asserted to be omnipotent; with many such subtle questions, inquiring— Can these be compatible with reason, and can you, as men of sense, believe them?" He then descanted on the superior merits of the Druidical religion, contrasting its "simple truth" with the "absurd fables told us by these foreigners;" concluding with a forcible and eloquent appeal to those who listened to him not to abandon the gods of their fathers, and go hankering after strange gods, especially such as were recommended by such baseless arguments and improbable tales as they had just heard.

When he concluded a murmur of applause agitated the assembly like a rustling of leaves in the forest, and the King said, "Venerable father, thou speakest well; thy words are those of truth; and it only remains to bid these strangers depart from our shores and return to the land from whence they have come, bearing with them our thanks for having come so far to teach us what they conceive to be the truth, but which we are unable to accept as consonant with reason."

In the vehemence of his oratorical action, the

Druid had caught up the skirt of his robe, and
the apostle had spied protruding therefrom a
cloven foot, and moreover that the heat issuing
therefrom had caused the upper part of the rock
on which it was placed to become partially
liquefied, or rather gelatinised, so that it adhered
to the foot. Suspecting, therefore, whom he had
to deal with, he cried out on receiving the order
to depart, " Hearken, oh King, I have told you
of the arch-enemy of God and mankind, who
tempted the first man to sin, and still goes about
luring men to perdition ; behold he—even he—
is present in this assembly, and has been
addressing you in advocacy of the false religion,
which you, in your ignorance, maintain. Him
will I unmask ; " and addressing himself to the
Druid, he cried in a stern and commanding voice,
" Satan, I defy thee ! in the name of the Saviour
of mankind, I command thee to display thyself in
thy proper person, and depart hence to the hell
from whence thou comest." In an instant, at
that adjuration, the Druid's robe and the
venerable beard fell from him, and he stood
revealed in all his hideous deformity, with a
malignant scowl on his countenance, and
springing up, he took flight, impregnating the

air with a sulphurous perfume, carrying with him a mass of rock, weighing several tons, which adhered to his foot.

At this unanswerable demonstration of truth of the religion proclaimed by the Apostles, the King, and even the Druids, became converted, and underwent the ceremony of baptism ; and the Apostles were empowered to go throughout Brigantium and preach the Gospel, which resulted in the conversion of multitudes, and the Brigantes became a Christian people.

Satan, however, although foiled so signally, set his wits to work to be avenged on the King for deserting his standard. He recollected the piece of rock which he had brought from Roulston and dropped in his flight some seven or eight miles from Iseur, the King's capital city, and this he resolved upon making use of to destroy that city. Accordingly he winged his way thither, and splitting up the rock fashioned it into four huge obelisk-like forms, and standing upon How-hill, he hurled them at Iseur, crying out :—

> "Borobrig, keep out of the way,
>   For Auldboro town
>   I will ding down."

It may be observed *en passant* that there is a

slight anachronism here, as Aldborough was not so called until the Saxon age, and Boroughbridge did not come into existence until after the Conquest. But that is a matter of not much consequence in a legend.

The stones which were thus intended to "ding down" the King's city were miraculously intercepted in their flight, falling and fixing themselves firmly in the earth between the city and the fords over the Ure (Boroughbridge), where three of them, still called "The Devil's Arrows," may be seen at this day.

The Giant Road-Maker of Mulgrave.

THE stately Castle of Mulgrave, now the home of the Phipps family— Marquises of Normanby—was built by Peter de Malo-lacu or de Mauley, in the reign of King John. Cox says, "he built a castle here for his defence, which, from its beauty and the grace it was to this place, he named it Moult-grace, but because it proved afterwards a great grievance to the neighbours thereabouts, the people, who will in such cases take a liberty to nickname places and things by changing one letter for another—c for v—called it Moult-grave, by which name alone for many ages it hath been and is now everywhere known, though the reason thereof is by few understood." A previous castle, with the barony, had been held by the de Turnhams, and the last male heir, Robert, having died without issue male, the barony and castle were inherited by his only daughter, Isabel, who, as was then the law respecting heiresses, became a ward of the Crown, and her hand at the disposal of the King. This Peter de Malo-lacu, or Peter of the Evil Eye, was a Poictevin of brutal and ferocious character, who was made use of by King John as the instrument for the murder of his nephew Arthur, for which piece of service he rewarded the murderer with the hand of the fair Isabel, with her inheritance.

But long before the de Mauleys and the de Turnhams, a noble Saxon family were lords of the surrounding domain, and dwelt in a castle on an eminence here, about three or four miles from the seashore at Whitby. Leland says (*temp.* Hen. 8), " Mongrave Castel standeth on a craggy hille, and on eche side of it is a hille far higher than that whereon the castel standeth. The north hille on the topp of it hath certain stones, commonly caul'd Wadda's grave, whom the people there say to have bene a gigant and owner of Mongrave." And Camden, " Hard by upon a steep hill near the sea (which yet is between two that are much higher) a castle of Wade, a Saxon Duke, is said to have stood; who, in the confused anarchy of the Northumbrians, so fatal to the petty Princes, having combined with

those that murdered King Ethered, gave battel
to King Ardulph at Whalley, in Lancashire, but
with such ill-sucess that his army was routed and
himself forced to fly. Afterwards he fell into a
distemper, which killed him, and was interred on
a hill here between two solid rocks, about seven
foot high, which being at twelve foot distance
from one another, occasions a current opinion
that he was of gyant-like stature."

It is with this Duke Wada that we are
concerned. He appears to have been a Saxon,
or rather an Anglian noble of considerable
consequence in the kingdom of Northumbria, and
to have taken a conspicuous part in the political
movements of that troublous period, when, as
Speed narrates, "the Northumbrians were sore
molested with many intruders or rather tyrants
that banded for the soueraintie for the space of
thirtie years." He was a man of gigantic stature
and a champion of redoubtable energy in war,
dealing death around him and cumbering the
field with the bodies of those who had fallen
beneath the blows of his ponderous mace. He
was indeed a true son of Woden in all respects,
excepting that he had relinquished the hope of
banqueting in the halls of the Walhalia, and appro-

priating the skulls of his enemies as drinking vessels; for through the influence of St. Hilda's Abbey of Streoneshalh, in the immediate vicinity, he had adopted the tenets of, if he did not regulate his life altogether according to, the principles of Christianity.

Now Wada was a married man, and had a helpmate of stature and proportions corresponding with his own. They were a well-matched couple, and seemed to have lived together in a state of ordinary connubial happiness, there being but one thing to disturb the even tenor of their lives, and that was that the lady had to go in all sorts of weather across a moor to milk her cows—a long and dreary journey even in summer, along the rough and stone strewn trackway, but more especially in winter, when the snow was frequently knee deep, and the bitter blasts of the north-east wind came careering over the sea and sweeping with relentless fury across the bleak and shelterless moorland.

Wada's Castle was a massive structure of stone, with round-headed unglazed windows, and a turret which commanded a fine outlook over the sea on one side, and the moorlands and Cleveland hills on the other. The rooms were of large size, as befitted the abode of a giant, but presented few of the appliances of comfort that are deemed commonplace essentials now-a-days. The walls were of bare stone, without drapery of any kind, and no ornamentation excepting some zigzag mouldings; the roofs were vaulted, and in those of large size supported at the intersections by one or more stunted round pillars; the windows were small, without glass, and furnished with wooden shutters to exclude the wind and rain in the inclement seasons of the year; and the furniture consisted of rough-hewn deal or oaken tables, and shapeless benches or stools, with an oaken coffer to hold valuables, and side shelves to hold wooden platters and vessels of earthenware. The fire in cold weather was made on the floor, of logs of wood or cuttings of peat, the smoke escaping as it could through the doorways or windows.

It was in such a room as this that Wada and his wife sat at breakfast, one rainy and boisterous morning. After devouring an enormous quantity of beef and swine's flesh, with manchets of oaten bread, washed down by repeated draughts of ale, Wada, wiping his mouth with the back of his hand, rose and went to look forth at the weather.

Wada was not a ferocious giant, dragging along half-a-dozen damsels, with one hand, by their hair, to immure them in his dungeons, and grind their bones to make his bread, as was the wont of the Cornish giants of old; nor was he, like them, stupid and weak-minded, so as to be easily outwitted and destroyed by the immortal Jack. On the contrary, although valiant in war, he abused not his great strength by tyrannising and oppressing his vassals, lived on good terms with his neighbours, and was gentle and tender in all his domestic relations. Hence, when he looked through his window and saw the sea foaming with wrath, and a few fisher-boats tossed about by the waves in their endeavour to gain shelter in Whitby Bay, and saw the sleet driving across the moor, he heaved a sigh, saying, "Methinks, sweetheart, thou wilt have a rough passage over the moor this morning; would to Heaven that it were not necessary for thee so to do." "I care not much," she replied, "for the falling rain and the boisterous wind, rough as they may be, but experience more inconvenience and suffering from the roughness of the road I have to traverse daily, so bestrewn is it with obstacles and stumbling-blocks, and so many bog-holes and quagmires have I to pass through."

Now it chanced that a short while before this Wada, in one of his wanderings, came upon the road constructed by the Romans, from Eboracum, by way of Malton to the Bay of Filey, and was struck by the facilities it gave for travelling, as compared with the more modern Saxon roads, if roads they could be called, which were mere trackways, formed and trodden down by the feet of men and animals. When his wife made the above reply, this recurred to his memory, and after a few minutes musing, the thought struck him -Why should not he make a road on this pattern for the benefit of his wife, whom he loved so dearly, and whose toil and labours he would be glad to lessen at any cost to himself?

After turning the matter over in his mind as to the practicability of the project, he came to the conclusion that it was perfectly feasible. There was plenty of material close at hand, in the shingle on the beach, and he had sufficient strength and energy to level the inequalities and fill up the boggy places, so as to make a firm foundation, and to spread over the whole a layer

of the stones gathered from the sea shore. Yes;
it was perfectly practicable, and could be
accomplished at the mere expense of a little
labour. He explained the project to his wife,
who was delighted with it, and undertook to
bring up the stones whilst he placed them in
position after forming the foundation.

They lost no time in commencing the work;
he with his spade in the levelling and bog-filling
operations, and she carrying up the shingle in
her apron; and it went on apace day after day
and week after week, soon presenting the
appearance of a newly macadamised road of
modern times, and was duly appreciated by Lady
Wada in her daily tramps across the moor.

It chanced that when the road was nearly
completed, in one of her journeys from the beach,
laden with shingle, her apron strings gave way
and her load fell to the earth, and there it was
left (some twenty cart-loads), and remained until
recent times as a monument of her industry and
strength, and an incontestable evidence of the
truth of the narrative. It was after this that
Wada joined in the insurrection against Ethelred,
the son of Moll, who, after his restoration from
exile, put to death the Princes Alfus and Alwin,

sons of King Alfwald, who were the rightful
heirs to the crown, and repudiated his wife to
marry Elfled, the daughter of Offa, King of
Mercia, "which things," says Speed, "sate so
neere the hearts of his subjects that they
rebelliously rose in arms, and at Cobre miserably
slew him, the 18th day of April, the yeare of
Christ Jesus, 794." After which Wada and his
confederates were defeated in battle by Duke
Ardulph, one of the aspirants to the Crown, and
fled to his castle, where he died of a terrible
disorder, and was buried, as stated, between two
huge stones.

The road leading from Dunsley Bay towards
Malton still exists, and goes by the name of
"Wada's Causeway," and one of the ribs of
Wada's wife is preserved in the present Mulgrave
Castle, but the present age is so incredulous
in respect to the chronicles of the past that
there are sceptics who assert that it is nothing
more than the bone of a whale.

Wada was the ancestor of the widely ramified
family of Wade, one of whom, at least—Marshal
Wade—inherited the road-making skill of his
ancestor. After the rebellion of 1715 he was
sent into the Highlands as military governor,

with the object of thoroughly subduing the
country and rendering it less available as a place
of refuge for rebels. With this view he
constructed a series of military roads, where
there had previously been only trackways, with
which the people were so delighted that they set
up a stone near Fort Augustus, with the
inscription :—

"If you had seen these roads before they were made,
    You would lift up your hands and bless General Wade."

The Virgin's Head of Halifax.

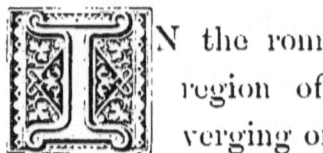N the romantic and somewhat sterile region of south-western Yorkshire, verging on the county of Lancaster, lies a valley, or rather what has the aspect of a valley, from its nestling under the shadows of some hills of considerable height. On the slope of an aclivity stands the modern town of Halifax, with its forest of lofty chimneys, its pretty park, and its many palatial structures, devoted to charitable and philanthropic purposes, due chiefly to the benevolence of the Crossleys, who, from a humble origin, have, within the memory of living persons, become manufacturing princes of the locality, and who, in consideration of their mercantile enterprise and the philanthropic use of the wealth they have acquired, have been honoured with a baronetcy. It is one of the most flourishing, or what Leland would term "quick," towns of the Yorkshire clothing district, and in recent times has increased rapidly

in population, wealth, and importance. It is not
even mentioned in Domesday-Book, nor does
its name appear in any record until the twelfth
century, when Earl Warren made a grant of the
church to the priory of Lewes, in Sussex.
About the middle of the fifteenth century it consisted of but thirteen houses, which during the
following hundred years increased to 520. In
1764, the parish, which, however, is very extensive, being seventeen miles in length by an
average width of eleven, contained 8,244 families;
and in 1811 the population numbered 73,815,
that of the town being 9,159, since which period
of eighty years it has been more than nontupled,
the census of 1891 giving the population at
82,900.

The town of Halifax owes its prosperity to its
mineral wealth. It is certainly not the place for
the agriculturist or the cattle breeder. In an
Act passed *temp.* Philip and Mary, it is recited,
" whereas the parish of Halifax, being planted in
waste and moors, where the ground is not apt to
bring forth any corn or good grass, but in rare
places and by exceeding and great industry of
the inhabitants; and the same inhabitants
altogether do live by cloth making, and the

F

greatest part of them neither getteth corn nor is able to keepe horse to carry wools, etc. ;" and Camden, in 1574, observes that there are 12,000 men in the parish, who outnumber the sheep, whereas in other parts we find thousands of sheep and but few men, " but of all others, nothing is so admirable in this town as the industry of the inhabitants, who, notwithstanding an unprofitable, barren soil, not fit to live upon, have so flourished in the cloth trade, which within these seventy years they first fell to, that they are both very rich and have gained a reputation for it above their neighbours, which confirms the truth of the old observation that a barren country is a great whet to the industry of the natives."

For the first three or four centuries after the Conquest, England was a great wool-growing but not a wool-manufacturing country. Sheep-breeding was a great source of income to the Cistercians, who, with all the private wool-growers, exported their produce to the spinners and weavers of the Low Countries. It was not until King Edward III., with great sagacity, foreseeing that England might manufacture as well as produce the raw material, and thus share in the profits arising out of that industry, invited over a number of Flemish artisans and settled them in Norfolk and Yorkshire, prohibiting the exportation of wool excepting under a tax of 50s. per pack. This was the foundation of the clothing industry of the West Riding, which has since then expanded so enormously; and Halifax was one of the first places to apply itself to the spinning and weaving of wool. As stated above, although poverty-stricken in an agricultural point of view, it possessed great mineral wealth in the shape of almost limitless deposits of coal, which was a valuable essential even in those primitive times, but which has become an absolute essential since the introduction of steam-power looms.

It is supposed that the manufacture was introduced into Halifax about the year 1414; but it was then on a very limited scale, and it was not until the beginning of the eighteenth century that the first great advance took place, by the erection of looms for the weaving of shalloons, everlastings, moreens, shags, etc., since which time damasks, and more recently still, carpets, have taken prominent places in the industries of the town; indeed, Halifax has absorbed a considerable portion of the trade which belongs legitimately to Kidderminster.

Although the town of Halifax is of comparatively modern origin, the name is unmistakably Saxon, indicating that previously to the Conquest there was a village or hamlet of some description to which that appellation was given. One tradition asserts that there was a hermitage dedicated to St. John the Baptist, in the valley, and that within it was preserved the face of the saint, which attracted vast numbers of pilgrims, and caused the name of the place of resort to be called Hali-fax, or Holy-face; and there may possibly be some substratum of truth in this, as the parish church is dedicated to the same saint. Dr. Whitaker partially adopts this theory, but his etymologies are frequently rather fanciful. He refers to this hermitage of St. John, "whose imagined sanctity attracted a great concourse of people in every direction, to accommodate whom there were four separate roads from different points of the compass, which converged in the valley, and hence the name Halifax, which is half Saxon and half Norman, signifying the Holyways, fax in Norman-French being an old plural noun, denoting highways."

Camden gives a brief outline of the legend given below, which he heard from the people of the vicinity, adding—" and thus the little village of Horton, or as it was sometimes called, 'The Chapel in the Grove,' grew up to a large town, assuming the new name of Halig-fax, or Halifax, which signifies holy hair, for fax is used by the English on the other side Trent to signify hair, and that the noble family of Fairfax in these parts are so named from their fair hair."

That the valley was esteemed a place of peculiar sanctity in the early ages is a matter of which there can be little doubt, and this is sufficiently evidenced by one fact alone. Within its precincts was born, about the end of the twelfth or beginning of the thirteenth century, John, the foremost mathematician of the age, author of "Tractatus de Sphœri Mundi," "De Computo Ecclesiastes," and "De Algorismo," who was honoured with a public funeral at the expense of the University of Paris, who assumed the name of Johannes de Sancto Bosco, or John of the Holy Wood. And here it may be incidentally noticed that the Holy Wood has since then produced other men upon whom the mantle of Johannes seems to have fallen. Here was born, in 1556, Henry Briggs, the eminent mathematician ; Gresham, Professor of Geometry, Savilian Professor at Oxford, and author of "Arithmetica Logarithmica," an improvement on Napier, containing logarithms of 30,000 natural numbers; Jesse Ramsden, the famous optician, and improver of the Hadley quadrant, who died A.D. 1800 ; and at Horton, seven miles distant, Abraham Sharpe, one of the best mathematicians and astronomers of his time, who died in 1742.

The shadows of evening were falling upon the valley, and the outlines of the rugged, verdure-less hills were gradually becoming more and more indistinct, as Father Aelred, having passed out of his little chapel of St. John the Baptist, where he had been performing the vesper service, proceeded to his lonely habitation, and after a simple meal of wild fruits and a draught of water from the little streamlet trickling down the hillside, sat him down to read for the hundredth time a transcript of a portion of Cædmon's Scriptural poems, after which he spent some time in prayer and self-communion, and then cast himself upon his sackcloth, which was spread over a layer of rough gravel, to slumber for a short time, in this mortifying and penitential fashion, to rise again at midnight for other devotional exercises.

Father Aelred was a man of thirty or thirty-five years of age, of pale countenance and emaciated frame, with sunken eyes and hollow voice, the result of rigorous fasting, long vigils, mortification of the flesh, and severe penitential exercises. In his boyhood he had been regarded, from his gravity of aspect, love of learning, and incipient piety, as one who was destined to become a light of the church of the coming generation, and was sent for his education to the famous School of Streoneshalh, established by the Lady Hilda, and at that time under the superintendence of her successor, the Princess Elfleda, where he imbibed Scriptural instruction from the lips of the then venerable Cædmon, a monk of the house. He became a novice of the house, passed the requisite examinations satisfactorily, and was in due course admitted as a fully accredited member of the fraternity. The strictness of his piety was such that he shortly found the life of a monk not to answer his longings for a higher life of holiness and a position where he could be of service to the souls

of his fellowmen.   He therefore left the shelter
of Whitby, and wandered about for some weeks,
until he came into the wild and barren-looking
mountainous district of the west, and finding
there a secluded valley, shut in by towering hills
and frowning rocks—a spot with a very sparse
and scattered population, and removed far away
from the noise and turmoil of the world—he
resolved to make it his home, and to settle down
in it as a hermit, shutting out all intercourse
with his fellowmen and women, save in the way
of imparting spiritual teaching and consolation to
the few simple unsophisticated rustics who dwelt
in the valley. He found a cavern in the
hill-side, which he enlarged and fashioned into a
habitation wherein to live ; fitting the entrance
with a door, to shelter him from the cold winter
winds and prevent the intrusion of wild animals,
above which he made an orifice for the admission
of light, which he glazed with a thinly scraped
sheet of horn, such as King Alfred's lanterns
were made of, and furnished the interior with
two sections of a tree trunk, the larger to serve
as a table, the smaller as a seat ; a shelf on which
he kept his eatables, with a knife, an earthen
platter, and a drinking horn, a piece of rough

sackcloth for his bed, and over it, fixed to the rock, a roughly-shapen cross, the emblem of his faith, beside which hung a knotted rope for the purpose of penitential flagellation. At a few rods distance he erected with his own hands, from timber cut by himself, a small chapel—a temple of God, sufficiently rude and unpretentious in point of architecture, but answering every purpose for which it was intended, that of a place of assembly for the simple and unlettered people of the valley, where they might join in the worship of God ; and here Aelred every evening performed divine service and catechised the small flock of which he had constituted himself the pastor, and on Sundays performed three full services, with a sermon and the administration of the sacrament of the Lord's Supper. And thus he came to be looked upon in the district as a most holy man, as indeed he was, and but little below a saint, who might be expected any day to commence the working of miracles, in the cure of the sick and afflicted.

There was one peculiarity about Aelred's character, which amounted almost to a mono-mania. He entertained a shrinking horror of fair-featured, beautiful women—not that there were many such in his solitary valley, they being, as a rule, embrowned by exposure to the sun, and their features corrugated by marks of rough toil and the troubles of life even from girlhood, and as such they experienced his sympathy and Christian charity; and the little children were always treated by him with tenderness and love, in imitation of his Divine Master, who had said " for of such is the kingdom of Heaven." But for the vain and frivolous of the sex, who seemed to deem nothing of supreme importance save the adornment of their persons, he felt profound scorn and contempt, mixed with a modicum of pity, and marvelled why they were sent into the world at all, unless, it might be, to test the virtue of man by the temptation of their fascinating allurements.

It happened, however, that not far distant a benevolent and wealthy lady had established a religious home for females. It was not exactly a nunnery, although it possessed many of the features of one, the inmates not being debarred from matrimony, although absolute chastity was an essential while resident there; nor were they garbed in unbecoming costumes, nor compelled to sacrifice that pride and ornament of woman, her

hair; besides which they were allowed a certain
amount of liberty in the way of visiting their
friends, which was not accorded to a regular
nun. The ladies of this establishment were wont
to go to Father Aelred to confess their little
peccadilloes, to which he saw no reasonable
objection, as they were generally very homely,
ill-favoured specimens of the sex, as is usually
the case with the inmates of nunneries, and thus
were in no way perilous to his chaste soul and
holy communings. Had they been otherwise, it is
probable that he might have declined the office
of father confessor to them, and closed the door of
St. John's Chapel against their intrusion.

It is a well-known psychological fact that the
body and the mind act and re-act upon each other
to their respective well-being or detriment, and
that if the one is neglected or abused the other
suffers in proportion; and this fact was evidenced
in the case of Father Aelred. As we have
observed, he was a man of intense and fervid
piety, the whole of his thoughts being con-
centrated on one sole object—the salvation of his
own soul and that of his fellow-creatures. Hence
he fasted for prolonged periods, denied himself a
sufficient measure of sleep, such as nature

demanded, subjected himself to severe self-flagellations, and in other ways outraged nature, fancying that by these mortifications of the flesh he was promoting the health of his soul. But the laws of nature are never broken with impunity, and he had to pay the penalty; instead of invigorating he impaired the powers of the spiritual portion of his dual entity, which, although distinct from, is essentially interwoven with the material half. At first he merely experienced lassitude, depression of spirits, and a harassing dread that after all his religious aspirations and rigid observance of the duties of the Church, he might find himself cast into the bottomless pit at last. These were followed by distressing dreams and visions of the Judgment Day, the frown and sentence of the arbiter of his eternal destiny, and the jeering scoffs of the enemy of souls, as he passed into the region of everlasting weeping and wailing. Deeming these to be proofs of the weakness of his faith and the languor of his religious life, he was led to redouble the rigour of his asceticism, the natural result being to intensify the malady he sought to cure. From seeing fearful visions in his dreams at night, he began to see horrible figures of demons by day, who crowded about him, with scoffing grimaces and leering looks, sometimes, as it seemed to his ears, as if uttering threats and sarcastic allusions to his assumed piety, or anon indulging in demoniac yells of laughter. Of course he attributed all these to the machinations of the devil, and prayed for deliverance from them; but he was haunted by them day and night, with increasing persistency, until at length the sanity of his mind gave way, and he became in fact a maniac, not, however, so pronounced as to render it evident to others, or prevent his performance of his priestly offices, nor did he relax his private devotional exercises.

On the evening above mentioned, when the holy father returned home from the chapel and sat down to the perusal of the transcript of Cædmon, which he had brought from Whitby, he was particularly disturbed in mind, and could not concentrate his thoughts upon what he was reading, which perpetually recurred at the evening service in the chapel and the advent of a new member of his congregation; besides which an imp had squatted himself on the table opposite him, and sat there grinning at him in a most diabolical fashion. It was the usual custom of the sisterhood of the religious house of which mention has been made to attend his evening service; and on this occasion a new member of the sisterhood was present for the first time. She had been just admitted as a novice, and was young and beautiful, with the fair, clear complexion, blue eyes, and long flaxen hair of the Anglian race, a striking contrast to the elderly, homely featured spinsters whom she accompanied. The moment he caught sight of her face, Aelred experienced a species of fascination, similar to that of the bird in the presence of the serpent, and although he battled with the feeling, he could not shake it off. To his eyes, she seemed like an angel come down from heaven, and the more he struggled to avert his thoughts from contemplating her celestial beauty, the more he felt impelled to turn his eyes again and again to where she sat. He felt it was wrong, so he brought the service to an abrupt close and hastened home to purify his soul, by prayer, from what he deemed the lust of the eye. But the vision was ever present in his mind's eye, so much so that he scarcely heeded or was conscious of the grinning imp on the table. He had retired to his sackcloth couch, after a wholesome application of the knotted rope and a prolonged prayer before the cross, and eventually fell asleep, but his dreams were all of the fair vision he had seen in the chapel, and for that night he was not haunted by his usual demon visitants.

A few days afterwards the Mother Superior of the little convent came to the chapel for confession, and brought with her her new daughter, to whom she introduced Aelred as her future father confessor, and it was with a strange unusual throbbing of his heart that he looked upon her fair form, as she bowed herself beneath his paternal greeting; but when he listened to her soft, silvery accents as she told him in confession her little sins of thought, his heart softened as it had never done before to any woman. These feelings, however, involuntary as they were, caused him much alarm, and he strove to banish them as being perilous to his soul, but it was impossible to drive the fair, and as he thought, angelic, image from his mind. A week passed by, to him a week of sad spiritual tribulation, for when in prayer his mind wandered away; nor was he able to fix his thoughts in contemplation, the angelic vision ever rising up to distract and perplex him.

One day when she came to confess she said to him—" Holy father, I have fallen into grievous sin ; I have made the probationary vow of abstraction from the world and of devotion to the sole service of God." " That is well, my daughter," said Aelred ; " persevere in that resolution, and God will bless you both now and for ever." " But, father," she continued, " I have suffered a fearful lapse ; I have looked back upon the world, and have almost regretted having taken the vows." " Backsliding," said Aelred in reply, " is, as you term it, a grievous sin ; but it is remediable by prayer, penitence, and fasting. But tell me more in detail the evil thoughts which have assailed your soul." " I almost fear to tell you," she answered. " Then can I not advise you in the matter excepting in general terms. Confide in me ; it is but speaking to God through me, and he will inspire me with words of remedial comfort ; otherwise I cannot grant absolution."

Thus urged, she stated that previously to entering the convent she scarcely knew what the passion of love meant, but since then it had sprung up in her heart with a vehemence that it seemed to be impossible to suppress. She had seen

one since she came into the valley, a pious and
godly man, who had at the first sight animated
her breast with the passion in so intense a degree
that it glowed and raged within her like a
furnace. The holy man at once concluded that
he himself was the person she referred to, and he
felt his heart beating wildly with an hitherto
unexperienced emotion, and at the same time his
brow became bedewed with perspiration, caused
by an apprehensive terror of the dangerous
position in which he found himself placed. He
stood silent and almost paralysed, looking down
upon her with fearful forebodings as to what she
would confess further, when she, wondering at his
silence, cast a furtive glance upward from her
hitherto downcast eyes. Everyone knows that
there is wondrous eloquence in the glance of a
female eye, and as her's met his, he felt at once
that it meant impassioned love—lawless love,
and it stirred up within his disordered mind all
the narrow bigotry of his sentiments in respect
to sexual love. He still stood silently gazing
upon her, when all at once a fearful idea flashed
across his mind, which caused him to pass at
once from a person of slightly distempered
intellect into a perfect madman. The idea was

that the girl before him was none other than Satan himself, who, not having been able to tempt him to sin by means of his imps in their repulsive demoniac forms, had assumed the semblance of a lovely virgin to allure him to carnal sin. Rising up to his full height, with eyeballs glaring and features distorted with indignant rage, he cried, "Satan, I know thee, and I defy thee; but no more shalt thou tempt man in that shape at least," and with that he dealt her a violent blow, and she fell senseless on the floor. "Ah!" cried he, "thou hast found thy match in me, but my work is not yet completed; thy head shall be placed aloft as a warning to others," and with that he procured a knife and severed her head from her body, which he then took out and fixed on the trunk of a yew tree, just where it begins to ramify, and when that was completed he rushed up the mountain with wild shouts of triumph and maniacal gesticulations.

The young novice not returning to the convent, search was made for her, and her headless body was discovered in the chapel, lying in a pool of blood, but it was not until the following day that the head was found fixed in the yew tree. On attempting to remove it, it was found that the long hair had taken root in the tree trunk, and was spreading downwards in thin filaments, and as this was looked on as a miracle, it was left there. Suspicion of the murder attached itself to the hermit-priest, and as he had been seen going up the mountain in a distraught state of mind, search was made for him in that direction, and his body was found at the foot of a precipice down which he had fallen, but whether through accident or for the purpose of suicide could never be known.

Camden says—" Her head was hung upon an ew-tree, where it was reputed holy by the vulgar, till quite rotten, and was visited in pilgrimage by them, every one picking off a branch of the tree as a holy relique. By this means the tree became at last a mere trunk, but still retained its reputation of sanctity among the people, who believed that those little veins, which are spread out like hair in the rind between the bark and the body of the tree, were indeed the very hair of the virgin. This occasioned such resort of pilgrims to it that Horton, from a little village grew up to a large town, assuming the name of Halig-fax, or Halifax, which signifies holy hair."

The Dead Arm of St. Oswald the King.

THE Anglian kingdom of Northumbria, of which York was the capital, presented in the seventh century one almost continuous series of battles and murders, massacres of the people, and desolation of the land. Ethelfrid, grandson of Ida, founder of the kingdom of Bernicia, and Eadwine, son of Ælla, founder of that of Deira, succeeded their fathers in their respective kingdoms about the same time; but the former, who had married Acca, Eadwine's sister, usurped his brother-in-law's throne and drove him into exile, who afterwards, by the assistance of Redwald, King of the East Angles, in the year 617, defeated and slew Ethelfrid in battle, and became King of Northumbria and eighth Bretwalda, or paramount monarch of Britain. He was converted to Christianity, and Penda, the pagan King of Mercia, in order to extirpate the heretical religion, invaded Northumbria, and defeated

Eadwine at Hethfield, who was slain in the fight. This happened in 633, and Penda then went into East Anglia on the same mission, leaving Cadwalla, a Welsh Prince, his ally, although a Christian, as Governor of Northumbria, who made York his headquarters, and ruled the people, especially those who had embraced Christianity and were the most devoted adherents of the family of Eadwine, with the most ruthless barbarity. On the death of Ethelfrid, his sons, Eanfrid and Oswald, fled into Scotland along with Osric, son of Ælfrid, King Eadwine's uncle, where they had been converted to Christianity under the teaching of the monks of Iona, or, as Speed puts it, " had bin secured in Scotland all his (Eadwine's) reigne, and among the Red-shanks liued as banished men, where they learned the true Religion of Christ, and had receiued the lauer of Baptisme." On hearing of the death of Eadwine, they returned to Northumbria, were welcomed by the people, and assumed the crowns —Osric of Deira, and Eanfrid of Bernicia. Cadwalla was still, however, potent in Northumbria, holding York and tyrannising over the people, and they were scarcely seated on their thrones when he slew Osric in battle, and caused

Eanfrid to be put to death when he came before him to sue for peace. Seeing that Christianity was almost extinct in the land, the people having reverted to the old faith, they both deemed it expedient to renounce Christianity and restore the worship of Woden, respecting which Bede says, " To this day that year (the year during which they reigned) is looked upon as unhappy and hateful to all good men ; as well on account of the apostasy of the English Kings, who had renounced the faith, as of the outrageous tyranny of the British King. Hence it has been agreed by all who have written about the reigns of the Kings to abolish the memory of these perfidious Monarchs, and to assign that year to the reign of the following King, Oswald, a man beloved of God."

Oswald was an altogether different man from his brother Eanfrid, a man of genuine faith, who had imbibed the true principles of Christianity, sincere in his devotions, and prepared to undergo any suffering, even death itself, rather than apostatise from what he was fully convinced was the truth. On the death of his brother he collected around him a small army of devoted followers, and with these advanced to meet

Cadwalla, relying on the justice of his cause, the bravery of his handful of men, and the assistance of God. He set up his standard, a cross, emblematic of his faith, at Denisbourne, near Hagulstad (Hexham), "and this done," says Bede, "raising his voice, he cried to his army, 'Let us all kneel and jointly beseech the true and living God Almighty, in his mercy, to defend us from the haughty and fierce enemy, for he knows that we have undertaken a just war for the safety of our nation.' All did as he had commanded, and accordingly, advancing towards the enemy with the first dawn of day, they obtained the victory, as their faith deserved." He adds, "In that place of prayer very many miraculous cures have been performed, as a token and memorial of the King's faith, for even to this day many are wont to cut off small chips from the wood of the holy Cross, which being put into water, men or cattle drinking thereof or sprinkled with that water are immediately restored to health." He then gives some instances, one of Bothelme, a brother of the church of Hagulstad, which was afterwards built on the spot, who broke his arm by falling on the ice, causing "a most raging pain," when he was given a portion of moss from the then old cross, which he placed in his bosom, and went to bed forgetting that he had it, but "awaking in the middle of the night, he felt something cold lying by his side, and putting his hand to feel what it was, he found his arm and hand as sound as if he had never felt any such pain."

Cadwalla was utterly defeated and slain, and his vast army (vast as compared with Oswald's small band of heroes) cut to pieces and dispersed. Having thus freed his country from the one disturbing element, he applied himself to its regeneration and restoration from anarchy and desolation to peace and good order. First and foremost, his object was the re-conversion of his people from the paganism into which they had lapsed, to Christianity, and to light afresh the lamp of truth, which had been almost altogether extinguished through the vigorous zeal of Penda on behalf of his ancestral gods of the north. With this object in view he sent to Iona for missionaries, to preach and teach throughout Northumbria, and Aidan was sent at the head of a body of monks, whose headquarters were fixed on the island of Lindisfarne, as resembling that of Iona, from whence they came, hoping to make it, like the latter, a centre of evangelical light to the mainland of Northumbria. Here they lived under the rule of Columba, the founder of Iona, in monastic seclusion, when at home, which was but seldom, as they were constantly on foot, staff in hand, tramping about through forests and moors and wild places of Oswald's kingdom. The King created a bishopric, to comprehend the whole of his territories, and constituted Aidan the first Bishop, who, it is said—such was the zeal of his subaltern monkish priests—baptised 15,000 converts in seven days. Besides this, the King caused churches and monasteries to be erected in various parts of his realm, and completed the church which King Eadwine had commenced at York, the forerunner of the magnificent fane which now adorns that city and is one of the most glorious specimens of Gothic architecture in England. Nor was Oswald less active in civil and secular matters, and in promoting the welfare of his people. He governed his kingdom with great wisdom and prudence, and under his peaceful sceptre the land was rapidly recovering from the effects of Cadwalla's desolating hand. He was the fifth King of Deira, ninth of Bernicia, third of Northumbria, and the ninth Bretwalda

or Supreme King of the island, " at which times
the whole Iland flourished both with peace and
plenty, and acknowledged their subjection vnto
King Oswald. For, as Bede reporteth, all the
nations of Britannie which spake foure languages,
that is to say, Britaines, Red-shankes, Scots, and
Englishmen, became subject vnto him. And yet
being aduanced to so Royall Majesty, he was
notwithstanding (which is maruellous to be
reported), lowly to all; gracious to the poore,
and bountifull to strangers."

It was a cold spring day; the sun shone
brightly, but imparted little warmth; the trees
were leafless, and the early flowers looked sickly
and languid, the effect of a long continuance of
north-easterly winds, which on this particular
day came coursing over the ocean, and were
roystering with boisterous glee and in fearful
gusts round the towers of Bamborough Castle,
and through the openings in the walls which
served the purpose of the glazed windows of after-
times. It was Easter-tide, and here King
Oswald had come from York, where he had kept
his Court, to celebrate this important festival of
the Church in the ancestral castle of his race.
The feast was laid in the banqueting-room, a

tolerably large but gloomy and, to nineteenth
century eyes, a wretchedly appointed apartment,
with but few of the appliances of modern comfort.
A fire of wood burnt on the hearth, the smoke at
times passing up the wide chimney, at others
driven inward by a down-current of the wind, and
sent in curling wreaths along the vaulted roof.
The room was lighted by means of narrow recessed
openings and arrow slits, useful in times of siege,
but inconveniently narrow for the admission of
light, yet wide enough to afford free entrance to
the chilling wind. The walls were of bare stones,
and the furniture a table of rough planks running
down the centre, with a smaller cross table, on a
sort of dais. At the latter table were seated
King Oswald, with his Queen Kineburga,
daughter of Kingils, the sixth monarch and first
Christian King of the West Saxons, on the one
hand, and Bishop Aidan on the other. Along the
other table sat some nobles and thegns, three or
four of the monks of Lindisfarne, and below these
the house carles and outdoor retainers of the
King's household. On the cross table was placed
a large silver dish filled with venison, wild boar's
flesh, and other dainties ; and distributed down
the long table were earthen dishes containing

meat of various kinds, wooden platters and knives, with drinking horns, and small loaves of barley bread; and on the table stood flagons of ale that had been brewed specially for the festival.

At the King's request the Bishop pronounced benediction on the food, with special reference to Him in whose memory the festival was celebrated, and who alone could administer the bread of life. He had scarcely finished, and the guests were beginning to handle their knives preparatory to an attack on the smoking viands, which gave forth a most appetising odour, when a sound as of a multitude of persons outside attracted their notice, and immediately after voices were heard : " In the name of Him who rose from the tomb this blessed morning, give us whereof to eat, that we starve not and die by the wayside." The King sent one of his house carles out to inquire who and what they were, who presently returned, saying that they were a band of some dozen mendicants, formerly well-to-do husbandmen, and their families, whose homes and crops had been destroyed by Cadwalla's followers, and that they were utterly destitute, deprived of the means of living, and dependent on charity for food until they could find means to replace themselves on their farms.

"Unfortunate creatures," exclaimed the King; "a fearful retribution awaits that so-called Christian prince in that world to which his crimes have sent him through our instrumentality by God's providence;" and, taking up the large silver dish, continued, "It is better that we celebrate not this festival, than that the poor of our realm die of starvation. Take this, Wilfrid, and portion out its contents among the famishing crowd, and when they have eaten, cut up the dish and distribute the fragments, that they may have the wherewithal to procure food on the morrow." Aidan, the Bishop, who was afterwards canonised, was struck with admiration at the pious and charitable act of the King, which he warmly applauded; and taking hold of his right arm, prayed that that arm and hand which had passed forth the dish might never become corrupt, but for ever remain fresh, in token and remembrance of this pious act of self-abnegation; and instead of feasting, this Easter day was spent by Oswald, his Queen, and the Bishop in fasting and prayer.

Penda, the pagan King of Mercia, was still

living, and still as inveterately hostile to the new
heresy as when he had made his raid on
Northumbria, and trampled it out by the defeat
and death of the Royal convert of Paulinus; and
now, when Oswald had been eight years on the
throne; had brought his kingdom, by wisdom
and good government, into a condition of peace
and prosperity; and had re-established Christianity on a sure and firm basis, he heard with some
dismay that the heathen King was muttering
threats against him, and gathering his forces
together for another invasion, and a second
suppression of the religion that sought the
dethronement of Woden as the god of heaven.
Yet although he heard these tidings with dismay,
he felt assured of the Divine protection, remembering how signally he had defeated Cadwalla
by fighting under the standard of the Cross,
despite the disparity of numbers. He remem-
bered, too, what miseries were inflicted on the
Northumbrians by the marching of hostile bands
to and fro, leaving, as they usually did, a desert
behind them strewn with the corpses of men,
women, and children; and he determined that,
rather than allow his people to be subjected again
to these sufferings, he would be beforehand with

the enemy and carry the war, with its resultant
ravages, into his own land. He therefore hastily
assembled his fighting men, and again uplifting
the standard of the Cross marched into Mercia,
his troops, like those of Cromwell a thousand
years afterwards, singing psalms and anthems as
they passed along.

Penda had collected together a large army,
and the rival hosts met at Masserfield, in the
modern Shropshire. They rushed towards each
other in mortal conflict, the one with shouts of
" Hallelujah !" the other with cries of " Aid us,
great Woden, thou mighty god of battle !" The
fight was long and obstinately contested, and
victory seemed to waver from one side to the
other until towards evening, when an arrow
struck Oswald and he fell to the ground, although
not mortally wounded ; but a cry arose amongst
his followers that he was slain, and, thinking that
their God had deserted them, they were stricken
with panic, threw down their arms, and fled in
every direction, hotly pursued by the Mercians,
who mercilessly killed all the fugitives whom
they overtook.

Although stricken down and faint from loss of
blood, Oswald still lived, and witnessed with

anguish of mind the cowardly and ignominious flight of his army. The Mercians came over the field, killing those of the fallen who were merely wounded; but when they came to Oswald they spared him, whom they had recognised, and brought him, with staggering steps and downcast heart, into the presence of their chief.

"Thou art he, then," said Penda, addressing him, "who darest to invade my dominions— the dominions of a descendant of Woden—thou, a worshipper of false gods!"

"It is even I," replied Oswald, in a weak voice; "I, Oswald, King of the Northumbrians, successor to the sainted Eadwine, who is now standing by the throne of the one true God, Jehovah, the God whom I worship, on whose arm I put my trust, and who, if He, in His inscrutable providence, hath delivered me up to thy cruel behests, will save my soul, that portion of me, my real self, which thou cannot touch, and bring me to dwell with Him for ever, in that heaven which thou canst never reach, unless thou repentest and abandonest thy false demon-gods, who can only conduct thee to the flames of hell."

"Blaspheming heretic," cried Penda, "I care

not for the heaven thou speakest of; sufficient for me will be the Halls of Walhalla, where, amid everlasting banqueting, I will use thy skull as my drinking-cup. Still, I will give thee one chance of life. Renounce thy false god; restore the worship of Woden in Northumbria, and thou shalt be replaced on thy throne as my tributary, whilst I, as monarch of Mercia, Northumbria, and East Anglia, extending from the Thames to the Forth, and from sea to sea, shall become the Bretwalda of Britain."

"Never, O King," replied Oswald "will I prove recreant to the truth. Thou mayest rend my sceptre from my grasp; thou mayest slay my kindred and massacre my people; thou mayest torture me, and put an end to my temporal existence; but never will I renounce that faith which affords me a secure hope of everlasting blessedness, whilst thou, if thou continuest the instrument of false gods, shalt be weeping and gnashing thy teeth in the torments of the bottomless pit."

"Then," roared out Penda, "thy death be on thy own head. Soldiers, hew the blasphemer to pieces!" And immediately he was stricken by half-a-dozen swords, and fell exclaiming,

H

"Lord Jesus, into thy hands I commend my soul."

The ferocious pagan, kicking the body with his foot as the last insult, gave directions for it to be cut into fragments, and scattered abroad to be devoured by birds of prey and the wild beasts of the forest; and his behests were at once carried into execution. And the birds and the beasts gathered together to the horrible carnival, and soon there was nothing left but the bare bones, saving one arm, which none of them would touch, and it remained entire and perfect as in life.

Some time after the battle of Masserfield the arm of the King was found, fresh and undecayed, and was conveyed to Northumbria and deposited in a magnificent shrine, where it remained uncorrupted for nine centuries, at first in the chapel of St. Peter, Bamborough Castle, and afterwards, when the Danes began to ravage the coast, in the monastery of Peterborough, whither it was removed, as Ingulphus informs us, for safety. The scattered bones were afterwards collected, by the pious care of Offryd, Oswald's niece, the daughter of Oswy, the illegitimate half-brother of Oswald, his successor on the throne of Northumbria, and slayer of Penda in battle.

She had become Queen of Mercia by her marriage with Ethelred, son and successor of Penda, who, after his father's death, had embraced Christianity. She placed the relics in the monastery of Bardney, in Lincolnshire, and his "standard of gold and purple over the shrine;" but when the Danes became troublesome in Lindsey they were removed to Gloucester, "and there, in the north side of the vpper end of the quire of the cathedrall church, continueth a faire monument of him, with a chappell set betwixt two pillers in the same church." At all these places—Masserfield, afterwards called Oswestry, after the martyr; at the place of burial of the relics; and at the shrines of the uncorrupted arm—throughout those nine hundred years some most wonderful miracles were performed, which are duly recorded in the pages of Bede and other writers; even a few grains of the dust which settled on the shrine of the arm, when mixed with water and drunk, were a sovereign specific for almost any disease.

Winwick, in Lancashire, disputes with Oswestry the claim of having been the place of St. Oswald's death, as there is St. Oswald's Well there; and from an inscription in the church it

appears to have been anciently called Masser-
felte ; moreover there is a tradition that he had a
palace there, which was within his dominions,
although his usual places of residence were
Bamborough and occasionally York.

The village of Oswaldkirk, near Helmsley,
derives its name from him, and there are several
churches in Yorkshire and elsewhere dedicated to
him.

The Translation of St. Hilda.

ST. Hilda was the nursing-mother of the infant Saxon Church ; the instructress of Bishops ; the preceptrix of scholars and learned men ; and the patroness of Cædmon, the first Saxon Christian poet—the Milton of his age. The Abbey over which she ruled with so much piety and prudence was, during her life and afterwards, one of the great centres of civilization and Christian light of the kingdom of Northumbria, and diffused its rays, beaming with celestial radiance, even beyond the bounds of that great northern monarchy.

She was a scion of the royal race of Ælla, the founder of the kingdom of Deira, or Southern Northumbria ; the daughter of Hererick (nephew of Eadwine, King of Northumbria), by his wife the Lady Breguswith ; was born in the year 614, and died in 680. She was converted to Christianity by the preaching of Paulinus, and was baptised along with her great-uncle and his court, in 627. Six years afterwards Eadwine was slain in battle by Penda, the heathen King of Mercia, and the nascent religion of Christianity stamped out, Paulinus flying for shelter with the widowed Queen and her children, to the court of her brother, the King of Kent. What became of Hilda during this period of anarchy we know not; but it seems evident that the afflictions and persecutions she underwent served only to deepen her faith and cause her to cling more closely to the Cross of Christ.

In 647, when she was thirty-three years of age, she resolved upon devoting her life entirely to the service of God, and with that view journeyed into East Anglia, where her nephew Heresuid reigned as King, and where her cousin, the pious Anne, resided. Her intention was to proceed hence to Chelles, in France, to join her sister, St. Herewide, who had retired to a nunnery there; but for some reason or other she lingered for twelve months in East Anglia. At the end of this period she was granted a plot of land on the Wear, upon which she erected a small house and resided there, in modest seclusion, for the space of a year, when the fame of her piety having spread abroad, she was appointed Abbess of

Hartlepool, a nunnery founded by Hein, the first woman who assumed the nun's habit in Northumbria, and who had now retired to the nunnery of Calcacceaster (Tadcaster). In her new capacity she set about her work with devoted zeal, regulating the discipline, reforming abuses, promulgating new and wholesome rules, and enforcing a strict attention to religious duties, in which she was aided by the counsels of her friend Aidan, Bishop of Lindisfarne, who, at the instance of King Oswald, had come from Iona to re-convert his subjects to the faith which had been trampled out by Penda.

In the year 642, Oswald, the second founder of Christianity in Northumbria, fell, like his predecessor Eadwine, under the ferocious sword of Penda, and was succeeded by Oswy in Bernicia, and Oswine in Deira; but in 650, Oswy caused the king of Deira to be murdered, and assumed the sceptre of Northumbria, north and south. Five years after this, Penda, with unabated zeal for his god—Woden—again made an inroad into Northumbria, with the intent of slaying the third Christian king of that realm. At first Oswy attempted to buy him off by bribes, but the Mercian potentate refused his offers, declaring that nothing would content him but the death of the King, and the utter extirpation of Christianity. "Then," said Oswy, "if the pagan will not accept our gifts, we will offer them to one who will--the Lord our God;" and he prepared for battle, making a vow that if God would vouchsafe him the victory he would erect a monastery, endow it with twelve farms, and dedicate his newly-born daughter to holy virginity and His service. With a comparatively small force, he marched against Penda, "confiding in the conduct of Christ," met him near Leeds, and, as the Saxon chronicle says, "Slew King Penda, with thirty men of the Royal race with him, and some of them were kings, among whom was Ethelhere, brother of Anne, King of the East Angles; and the Mercians became Christians."

This great and decisive victory, the last conflict in England between heathendom and Christianity, was the turning-point in Hilda's career of eminence. Had Penda again been the victor, Northumbria would again perhaps have lapsed into paganism, and the future saint never have been heard of beyond the vicinity of Hartlepool.

As it was, King Oswy, mindful of his vow,

erected a monastery at Streoneshalh, on the bank
of the Esk, where it falls into the sea in Whitby
Bay. It was placed on a lofty headland, with a
steep ascent from the little fishing hamlet at its
foot and a precipitous escarpment to the sea. It
was formed for both male and female recluses,
and the fame of Hilda for piety and judicious
government was such that she was selected by
the King as the most fitting for the government
of the establishment. Under her rule
Streoneshalh became not only a model monastic
house, but a great school of secular and theological learning. During her superintendence,
not less than five of her scholars attained the
mitre, all of them illustrious prelates of the
Saxon Church—St. John, of Beverley; St.
Wilfrid, of Ripon; and Bosa, Archbishops of
York; Hedda, Bishop of Dorchester; and
Oftfor, Bishop of Worcester. "Thus," says
Bede, "this servant of Christ, whom all that
knew her called 'mother,' for her singular piety
and grace, was not only an example of good life
to those that lived in her monastery, but afforded
occasion of amendment and salvation to many
who lived at a distance, to whom the fame was
brought of her industry and virtue." Fuller

observes, " I behold her as the most learned
female before the Conquest, and may call her the
she-Gamaliel at whose feet many learned men
had their education." During her Abbacy, the
famous Synod, convened by King Oswy, was
held within the walls of Streoneshalh, to settle
the vexed questions of the time for the celebration
of Easter, and of the tonsure, which were subjects
of warm dispute between the ancient British
Church and that of Rome, the Northumbrians
adhering to the former, as inculcated by the
missionary monks of Iona, who had been brought
hither by Oswald, and who now occupied the sees
of York and Lindisfarne. The King, who had
been educated in Scotland, and consequently held
to the British modes, presided, whilst his son,
Prince Alfred, who had been in Rome, supported
the Romanist views.

On the British side were ranged the Abbess
Hilda, Colman, Bishop of Lindisfarne, and the
venerable Cedd, Bishop of the East Saxons; on
the Romanist, Agilbert, Bishop of the West
Saxons, Wilfrid of Ripon, then a priest, Romanus,
and James the Deacon. The dispute was settled
in favour of the Romish rule, chiefly through the
eloquence and force of argument of Wilfrid, who

afterwards made so conspicuous a figure in the Northumbrian Church; and Colman, with his British clergy returned to Iona. The Abbess was as famous for miracles as for her other qualities. On the coast of Whitby are found great numbers of specimens of the petrified Cornu Ammonis, commonly called snake stones, resembling as they do coiled-up snakes, without heads. This is how their origin is accounted for. When the Abbey was first built, the neighbourhood was infested by snakes, which were a great annoyance to the brethren and sisters of the monastery, and the Abbess, by means of prayer, caused them all to be changed into stone.

> " And how, of thousand snakes, each one
>   Was changed into a coil of stone
>   When holy Hilda prayed :
>   Themselves, within their holy bound,
>   Their stony folds had often found,
>   They told how sea fowls' pinions fail,
>   As over Whitby's towers they sail,
>   And, sinking down, with flutterings faint,
>   They do their homage to the saint."

The Abbess founded some cells in divers places dependant on the Abbey, one of which was at Hackness, near Scarborough, which she made use of as a retreat from the bustle and cares of

Streoneshalh, where she could, undisturbed, devote her time more strictly to the exercises of fasting, prayer, and meditation, returning to her duties at the Abbey refreshed and invigorated spiritually, and the better enabled to undergo the distractions incident to her position as head of a community of differing and often perplexing temperaments. To these cells also she frequently sent her nuns, to give them an opportunity for cultivating closer communion with God, for their spiritual edification.

For the last six years of her life the Abbess suffered greatly from severe indisposition, which frequently laid her prostrate for weeks together, "Yet during all this time she never failed to return thanks to her Maker, or publicly and privately to instruct the flock committed to her charge, admonishing them to serve God in health, and thank Him for adversity or bodily infirmity."

Among the nuns under her care was one from Ireland named Bega, who was most exemplary in her attention to the duties of her religious calling, eminently endowed with spiritual grace, and conspicuous for her humility, self-abnegation, and all the virtues which adorn a Christian life; which qualities endeared her to the venerable

Abbess, and they came to regard each other as mother and daughter rather than as Lady Superior and ordinary nun of a religious establishment.

During the long illness of the Abbess, Bega was her constant attendant and nurse, and accompanied her in her occasional retreats at Hackness. One afternoon they were seated together in the Abbess's private room, when the invalid seemed to be rallying in health and entering upon one of her alternate periods of comparative convalescence. Bega had been reading to her a new paraphrase of a portion of the Bible, the composition of Cædmon, the cow-boy poet of Streoneshalh. She laid down the manuscript at the conclusion, expressing a hope that the Abbess had not been wearied by her imperfect reading, and that in spite of defective knowledge of the characters on the part of the reader, she had been enabled to follow the sense and appreciate the beauty of the rendering.

"Nothing from the pen of Cædmon," said the Abbess, "ever wearies me; on the contrary, his compositions are so redolent of spiritual beauty that they seem to refresh my soul, and invigorate my body as well. Indeed, at this moment I feel so much better in health that if no relapse occurs in the interval, I propose on the morrow relieving our good Prioress from the duties which I have delegated upon her during my sickness."

"Happy am I," replied Bega at hearing this, "and I trust that God, if he sees fit, may preserve you for many years to come, in the superintendence and guidance of this holy house. But, mother dear, your restoration of bodily strength emboldens me to solicit a boon."

"What is it my dear child? Anything that I can grant shall be yours. I promise this without knowing what you wish, feeling assured that you will solicit nothing that is inconsistent either with your maidenly character or with your altar-made vows."

"I pray for nothing unbeseeming my character in such respects; but, holy mother, of late I fear I have experienced some spiritual declension, and that I have become more carnally minded than becomes one whose thoughts should be centred on Christ alone, and I pray you, mother dear, to permit me to retire into more entire seclusion from the world, that I may, by abstinence, prayer, and close communion with God, be restored to a more wholesome frame of soul."

"Your boon is granted, my child, gladly; repair at once to Hackness, and may God shed his blessing upon your pious aspiration for a higher life of holiness."

The following day Bega was escorted to the cell, where the Abbess, with an almost Cistercian eye for sylvan beauty, had planted it, that in the midst of a natural Paradise it might bloom as a spiritual Eden, and there she at once commenced a season of wholesome asceticism and religious exercises.

A week passed away, and Bega, absorbed in her devotional exercises, had become emaciated by the rigour of her fasting without heeding it; and as is usual in such cases, her spirit had become more etherealised and more susceptible of supernatural influences. After vespers one evening she returned to her lonely sleeping apartment, a bare and scantily furnished room, and lay down on her bed, consisting of a thin layer of straw on a hard, wooden pallet, with nothing more than a coarse rug for her coverlet. She slept for a short space, then awoke and rose to repeat the nocturnes, kneeling on the rough flooring stones. She then lay down again and composed herself to sleep, and was in the half-

conscious state between sleeping and waking
when she was aroused by hearing a passing-bell
boom forth, which sounded like that of Streoneshalh, which was miles beyond earshot, and was
the more remarkable as the bell of Hackness was
much smaller and altogether different in tone.
She listened with soul-thrilling awe, and thought,
" Can it be that the holy mother is departing at
this moment to her heavenly rest, and that the
sound of the passing-bell is miraculously brought
to mine ears ? "   Scarcely had the thought flashed
across her mind, when, looking upward, the
vaulted roof seemed to be melting away, like a
mist under the influence of the morning sun.   In
a very short space of time it disappeared
altogether, and there was presented to the eye of
the gazer the expanse of sky studded with stars,
sparkling like clusters of diamonds.   Presently
the knell of the passing-bell ceased.   And there
broke upon her ear the sound of distant vocal
music.   As it came nearer, it seemed different
from any music she had ever heard ; unearthly ;
heavenly ; so ravishingly sweet was the melody.
The words she was unable to comprehend, but
there was something about them which seemed to
declare them of celestial origin.   With raptured

ears she listened as the choir, which appeared to
be floating in the air, came on and on until it
sounded as if immediately overhead. All
this while, too, a constantly increasing effulgence
of supernatural light was diffusing itself over the
firmament, and when the music came into close
proximity to the cell, there burst upon her sight
a vision, the glory of which she could have
hitherto formed no conception of. It was that of
a convoy of angels, fairer and more lovely in form
and feature than anything ever conceived by
artist or poet, or than ever trod the earth. It
was they who were chanting the divine melody
as they floated along overhead with an upward
tendency; and in their midst was the beautified
soul of the sainted mother of Streoneshalh, which
they were escorting to the everlasting realms of
purity and peace; of eternal rest, and an endless
duration of unalloyed happiness. The rapt eyes
of Bega were not allowed to rest long on this
celestial vision; the group ascended higher and
higher; the voices became fainter and fainter,
until they were altogether lost; and Bega
overcome with emotion, fell into an ecstatic
trance, and when she awoke from it there
was nothing to be seen but the glimmer of

I

the moonshine on the walls and roof of her cell.

The next day a messenger arrived announcing the death of the Abbess, which he stated occurred immediately after nocturnes on the preceding night.

Bega remained a little while at Streoneshalh, and then went into Cumberland, and provided a religious house, called after her, St. Bees, where she spent the remainder of a most holy life.

A Miracle of St. John.

TWO thousand years ago, what is now the East Riding of Yorkshire was chiefly forest land, with the exception of the Wold uplands, which were pastures, almost destitute of trees, having some semblance to the swelling and rolling waves of the ocean, where the Brigantes fed their flocks and herds, where they dwelt in scattered hamlets, and where they now sleep in their multitudinous tumuli. In the lowlands at the foot, the forest was very dense, and was the home of wolves, boars, deer, and other wild animals, which were hunted by the natives, who fed upon their flesh and clothed themselves with their skins. This was called the forest of Deira, and in one spot by the river Hull, a few miles distant from the Humber, was a cleared space, with an eminence in the midst, and at its foot, extending westward, a pool of water, afterwards a marsh or moor, and since drained, forming now a portion of the town of

Beverley, its former condition being indicated by
two parallel streets—Minster-moorgate, the
place of the moor by the Minster; and Keldgate,
the place of springs. This was a Druidical
open air temple, where the mystical rites of
Druidism were performed.

When the primitive Christian religion was
introduced into Britain, it is presumed that a
Christian church was established here, on the
rising ground by the lake, as the early Christians
built their churches, where practicable, on spots
held sacred by the people, which supposition
seems to be confirmed by the express statement
that St. John rebuilt, not built, the church in
Deira Wood. This early church, doubtless a
very rude affair of timber and thatch, was
destroyed or allowed to fall into ruin when the
Saxons and Angles overspread the land and
replaced the religion of Christ by that of Odin.
It might possibly be repaired during the short
period after the second introduction of Christianity by Paulinus and the conversion of King
Eadwine, but, if so, would be again destroyed a
few years after, under the desolating hands of
Penda of Mercia, and Cadwalla, as it lay in ruins
until the beginning of the eighth century, when

it was restored on a grander scale by John, Archbishop of York.

St. John, the learned and pious prelate, one of
the brightest luminaries of the Saxon Church,
was a member of a noble Saxon family, a native
of Harpham on the Wolds. He was born in the
year 640, studied in the famous Theological
School of St. Hilda at Streoneshalh, and became
successively Bishop of Hagulstat (Hexham) and
Archbishop of York, which latter see he held,
with unblemished reputation and great usefulness,
for a period of more than thirty-three years.

He was almost incessantly employed in going
about his vast diocese, rectifying abuses,
regulating disordered affairs, exhorting the lax,
and commending the faithful. In one of these
visitations he came to the place in the forest of
Deira which had been, half a millennium
previously, the Llyn-yr-Avanc of the Celts, and,
according to some antiquaries, the Peturia of the
Romans, a conjecture which is supported by the
discovery of a tesselated pavement and other
Roman remains, where he found the ruins of the
old primeval British Church. The beauty and
seclusion of the spot struck him as being
eminently fitted for the establishment of a

monastery, and probably the thought flashed across his mind that hither he would like to retire, in his declining years, to finish his life, after the cares and anxieties of his prelateship, in the calm of cloistered existence and in the company of a pious brotherhood.

He did not allow the idea to pass away from his thoughts, but soon after made arrangements for carrying it out. He rebuilt the choir of the old church, founded a monastery of Black Monks, of the order of St. Columba, and an oratory for nuns, south of the church, which afterwards was converted into the parish church of St. Martin; erected the church of St. Nicholas, in the manor of Riding; placed seven secular priests and other ministers of the altar in the head church, and appointed Brithunus the first Abbot of the monastery, with superintendence over the other establishments. In 717, he resigned his see, being then feeble and oppressed by the infirmities of age, and retired to his monastery, where he died in 721, and was buried in the porch at the eastern end of the church.

After St. John, the next greatest benefactor to the church and town of Beverley was Athelstan the Great, King of Saxon England. Indeed, he

may be considered the founder of the secular,
as St. John was of the ecclesiastical, town. The
town and church had been destroyed by the
Danes in 867, but a few years after the dispersed
canons and monks returned, and repaired, as far as
they could, their ruined buildings, so as to be
able to continue the celebration of the services;
but they remained in a dilapidated state for
nearly half a century, when Athelstan laid the
foundations of the future grandeur of the church,
and of the commercial importance of the town.
He had heard of the sanctity of St. John, and
the wonderful series of miracles he had performed,
both during his life and after his death, and
having occasion to chastise Constantine, King of
Scotland, for abetting the Danish Anlaf of Northumbria in an invasion of that portion of his
dominions—for he had by conquest added
northern England to his government, and was in
truth the first King of England, rather than
Egbert—he visited Beverley on his march to
Scotland, and implored the aid of the Saint,
leaving his dagger on the altar as a pledge that,
if successful, he would bestow princely benefac-
tions on the church and town. By the assistance
of St. John, who appeared to him in a vision, he

was the victor in the decisive battle of Brunnan-
burgh, and nobly he kept his word. He made the
church a college of secular canons; endowed it
with four thraves of corn from every plough in
the East Riding; and made it a place of
sanctuary, as a refuge for criminals, with a stone
frid-stool, still in the Minster. He granted a
charter to the town, constituting it the capital of
the East Riding, with many privileges and
extraordinary rights; in consequence of which
opulent merchants flocked to the town, and it
soon began to flourish mightily, and became one
of the wealthiest and most important of the trading
towns of the realm. He also assigned the manor
to the Archbishops of York, who built a palace
there on the south of the church; vied with each
other in their patronage of the town, and
in adding to and endowing the collegiate
church.

In the beginning of the eleventh century
Archbishop Puttock added a chancellor, a
precentor, and a sacrist to the establishment,
and erected a costly shrine for the relics of St.
John, to which they were translated with great
pomp in 1037. Archbishop Kinsius erected a
western tower to the church, and Aldred, who

held the see at the time of the Conquest, rebuilt
the choir, and ornamented it with paintings and
other decorative work, completed the refectory
and dormitory of the monastery, and increased
the number of canons from seven to eight,
changing them at the same time from canons to
prebendaries.

At this time—the period of the Conquest and
of the legend—we may assume from the usual
characteristics of the church architecture of the
time, that the church was an oblong building of
two stories, divided into a nave and chancel, with
a low tower at the western end. There would
probably be a lower and an upper range of
circular-headed windows, with doorways of the
same character, decorated with zigzag mouldings,
and in the interior would be a double row of
massive stunted columns, supporting semi-circular
arches, and at the eastern end, in the chancel,
the superb shrine of St. John, which was
attracting pilgrims from all parts, and was
beginning to be encrusted with the silver and the
gold and the gems, bestowed for that purpose by
the pilgrims in grateful remembrance of wonderful
cures effected upon them by the miracle working
of the saint. Such would most probably be the

church in which occurred the incidents narrated in our legend.

When the Norman Duke William had won the battle of Hastings, and subdued southern and mid England, and had been crowned King in the place of the slain Harold, he discovered that he was not really King of England, but of a part only—that portion north of the Humber, forming the old Saxon kingdom of Northumbria of the Heptarchy, and one of the Vice-Royal Earldoms of Saxon England, continuing to maintain its independence with stubborn tenacity; and it was not until after much bloodshed that he overcame the sturdy Northumbrians of a mixed Anglian and Danish race, and garrisoned York, the capital, with a Norman garrison to keep the province in subjection. No sooner, however, was his back turned than the people, under Gospatric, Waltheof, and other Danish and Saxon leaders, broke out afresh in insurrection, massacred the Norman garrison at York, and vowed to drive that people and their Duke, the usurper of Harold's throne, from Northumbria at least, if not from England altogether. It was after one of the most formidable risings that the Conqueror swore that "by the splendour of God" he would utterly destroy and exterminate the Northumbrians, so that no more rebellions should rise to trouble him in that quarter of his dominions; and with this view he marched northwards, crossed the Humber— probably at Brough —and encamped at a spot some seven miles westward of Beverley, purposing to proceed henceward to York on the morrow.

On his road from the Humber to his encampment he had burnt the villages and crops, and slain the villagers who came in his way, but the majority, taking the alarm, fled to Beverley, hoping to find safety within the limits of the League of Sanctuary, thinking that even so merciless a soldier as Duke William would respect its hallowed precincts. But he, godly in a sense, and superstitious as he was, entertained no such scruples, and he had no sooner seen his army encamped than he despatched Thurstinus, one of the captains, with a body of Norman soldiers to ravage and plunder the town.

The people of Beverley and the fugitives who had fled thither deemed themselves safe under the protection of their patron saint; nevertheless they felt some alarm when the news was brought that the ruthless Conqueror lay so near them, and still more when they heard that a detachment was marching upon the town with hostile intentions. The church was filled with devotees, who prostrated themselves before the saint's shrine, imploring him not to abandon his church and town in this extremity. The day had been gloomy and downcast, but when they were thus supplicating the holy saint the sun came shining through one of the windows directly upon the shrine, and lighted it up with a brilliance that seemed supernatural, which was looked upon as a favourable response to the prayers of the supplicants.

Thurstinus and his followers had by this time entered the town, but had, so far, done no injury to either person or property. As they approached the church, they perceived before them a venerable figure, clad in canonical raiment, with gold bracelets on his arms, moving across the churchyard, towards the western porch. The sight of the golden bracelets excited the cupidity of one of the subalterns of the corps, who darted after him, sword in hand, and overtook him just as he was passing through the portal. The soldier had but placed his foot within the church, when the aged man turned

towards him and exclaimed, "Vain and presumptuous man! darest thou enter my church, the
sacred temple of Christ, sword in hand, with
bloodthirsty intent? This shall be the last time
that thine hand shall draw the sword," and
instantly the sword fell from his grasp, and he
sank down on the ground, stricken by a deadly
paralysis. Thurstinus, not witting what had
happened to his officer, came riding up, with
drawn sword, with the intent of passing into the
church to despoil it of its valuables; but on
entering the doorway he was confronted by the
aged man with the bracelets, who stretched forth
his arm, and said to him, "No further, sacrilegious man; wouldst thou desolate my church?
Know that it is guarded by superhuman power,
and thou must pay the penalty of thy impious
temerity!" and immediately he fell from his
horse to the pavement with a broken neck, his
face turned backward, and his feet and hands
distorted "like a misshapen monster." At this
manifest interposition of Heaven the Normans
fled back to the encampment with terror-stricken
countenances, and the people in the church
looked round for their deliverer, but he had
vanished, and they then knew that it was St.

John himself, who had come down from heaven to protect his town and church from the insult and ravages of Norman ferocity.

When the soldiers reached the camp they reported to their superior officer the result of their expedition and the horrible death of their leader, which they could not attribute to anything less than supernatural power. The report in due course reached the King, who summoned the soldiers into his presence, and listened to their narrative with superstitous awe. "Truly," said he, "this John must be a potent saint, and it were well not to meddle with what appertains to him, lest worse evil befal us. He may possibly use his influence in thwarting our designs against the rebels of this barbarous northern region. Let not his town and the lands pertaining to his church be injured, or subject to the chastisement and just vengeance we intend against those who have dared to raise the standard of revolt against our divinely ordained authority; but rather let them be protected, for it were bootless and perilous to fight against Heaven. Onward then to York, and when we have, by such severity as the case warrants, effectually crushed the spirit of revolt, we will consider what further can be done to propitiate this saint, whom it were well to conciliate by gifts, so that he may be led in gratitude to recompense us by assisting in the consolidation of our power, which is not yet established on sufficiently firm foundations."

He found no difficulty in suppressing the insurrection when he reached York, putting to the sword those of the insurgents who remained there after their leaders had fled towards Scotland. In order to prevent any future rising, with any possible chance of success or gleam of hope, he then meditated and carried out a cold-blooded scheme, which might have been deemed a measure of policy, but which for ferocity equalled any act of cruelty perpetrated by the most atrocious tyrant of pagan ages. He sent forth his men with swords and torches, to the north, the west, and the east, and for an extent of sixty miles, from York to Durham, by several miles in breadth, laid the country desolate. Villages, churches, monasteries, and castles, with the granaries of corn and the standing crops, were all destroyed by fire, and every person, man, woman, child, or priest, met with was slaughtered without mercy; and when the work had been accomplished, this vast extent of country bore the aspect of a Western American prairie after it had been swept by fire, leaving only the charred stumps of the trees standing, with this difference, however, that there only the half-burnt bodies of animals, such as were not able to escape by flight, are found; whilst here, scattered profusely on the wood-side, and round their once cheerful and happy homesteads, lay the rotting and putrefying corpses of human beings, on which the wolves and birds of prey were battening and gorging themselves; and it took many and many a year before this region recovered itself and became again a country of farmsteads and villages, of crops and fruit trees, and of an industrious population. William of Malmesbury says that not less than 100,000 persons perished in this fearful act of vengeance; and Alured of Beverley, a monkish writer, and treasurer of St. John's Church, states that "The Conqueror destroyed men, women, and children, from York even to the western sea, except those who fled to the church of the glorious confessor, the most blessed John, Archbishop, at Beverley, as the only asylum." An indisputable proof of the desolation wrought on the lands appears in the Domesday Book, which in most places in

Yorkshire is described as waste or partially waste, and which is represented as of no value or of much less value than in King Edward's time; whilst in Beverley and the lands of St. John there is scarcely any waste mentioned, and the value is given as the same or nearly the same as in the reign of the Confessor. Under Bevreli we read, "Value in King Edward's time, to the Archbishop 24 pounds, to the Canons 20 pounds, the same as at present."

The King not only exempted the town and demesne from devastation, but became a notable benefactor thereto. He added to the possession of the church certain lands at Sigglesthorne, and granted the following confirmatory charter:—
"William the King greets friendly all my Thanes in Yorkshire, French and English. Know ye that I have given St. John at Beverley sac and soc over all the lands which were given in King Edward's days to St. John's Minster, and also over the lands which Ealdred, the Archbishop, hath since obtained in my days, whether in this Thorp or in Campland. It shall all be free from me and all other men, excepting the Bishop and the Minster priests; and no man shall slay deer, nor violate what I have given to Christ and St.

K

John. And I will that there shall be, for ever, monastic life and canonical congregation so long as any man liveth. God's blessing be with al Christian men who assist at this holy worship. Amen."

And from this time the town flourished greatly, and grew rapidly in population and wealth. As to the church, it became more than ever the resort of pilgrims, who left rich presents on the shrine of St. John. In the year 1188 the old Saxon church was destroyed by fire, which may be deemed a fortunate occurrence, as men were stimulated at this, the best period of Gothic architecture, to erect over the relics of St. John a structure worthy of his eminence and fame; and the outcome of this impulse was the uprising of the existing magnificent church, which is now the great architectural glory of the East Riding.

The Beatified Sisters of Beverley.

N the south aisle of the nave of Beverley Minster may be seen an uninscribed canopied altar tomb. It is a very fine specimen of the Early Decorated style, manifestly dating from the period of Edward II. or the earlier portion of the reign of his successor. It is covered with a massive slab of Purbeck marble, rising above which is an exquisitely proportioned pointed arch or canopy, with pinnacles and turrets, crocketted work and finials, all elaborately chiselled and carefully finished. History records not whose mortal remains are deposited in the tomb: there it stands like the Sphynx on the sands of Egypt, maintaining a mysterious silence as to its origin, "a thing of beauty," displaying its elegance of form and the charms of its sculptured features to all beholders; but seeming to say—"Admire the perfection of my symmetry if you will, but inquire not whose relics I enshrine, whether of

noble or saint. Unlike my more gorgeous sister tomb, in the choir, near the altar, which blazons forth the glory of the Percys, I choose, with Christian humility, and recognising the fact that death renders all equal, and that in the sight of the Almighty Judge a Percy is no better for all his glories than the pauper—to draw a veil over the earthly greatness of the family to which I belong."

Although history is thus silent in respect to the origin of the tomb, tradition is less reticent, and from its oral records we learn, not perhaps all that can be desired, but a narrative that probably has a basis of truth.

About a mile westward of Beverley Westwood, on the road to York, lies the pretty picturesque village of Bishop Burton, with its church on an eminence commanding an extensive view of the Wold lands on one hand, and of the country sloping down to the Humber on the other. It is environed by groups of patriarchal trees, including a noble specimen of the witch elm on the village green, with a trunk forty-eight feet in circumference, and which is held in great veneration by the villagers; and in the valley below is a small lake, which doubtless supplied fish to the house-

hold of the Archbishops of York when they had
a palace here. It is a very ancient village, dating
from the Celtic period, when it formed a
burial place of the Druids and British chieftains.
One of the numerous tumuli was opened in 1826.
It was seventy yards in circumference, and was
found to contain several skeletons of our remote
forefathers of that race. From some tesselated
pavements which have been discovered, it appears
also to have been occupied afterwards by the
Romans.

At the end of the seventh and beginning of
the eighth century, the Lordship of South
Burton, as it was then called, was held by Earl
Puch, a Saxon noble. Its name was changed,
after the Conquest, to Bishop Burton, from the
circumstance that it belonged to the Archbishops
of York, and their having a palace in the village,
where Archbishop John le Romayne died in
1295. At this time South Burton formed a sort
of oasis in a vast wilderness of forest, extending
for miles in every direction, including the now
open breezy upland of Beverley Westwood, then
infested by wolves, through which ran trackways
to Beverlega, where stood the recently founded
church and monastery of St. John, northward of

which, at the foot of the Wolds, lay another extent of forest land, called Northwood, perpetuated to this day in the name of the street —Norwood. Earl Puch's mansion was an erection of timber, with few of the appliances of modern domestic life, with a large hall, wherein he dined with his family and guests at the upper end of a long table, and his retainers and domestics at the lower end. More in the interior were the Lady Puch's bower and other private and sleeping apartments of the family; with inferior rooms for the household servants, the swineherds, cowherds, huntsmen, and other outdoor menials sleeping in the outhouses, with the animals of which they had charge.

Earl Puch had built a church in the village, a very primitive specimen of architecture, consisting of nave and chancel, of timber and wattles, with round-headed doors and windows, and rude zig-zag ornamentation. It had neither tower nor transept, lacked bells, and its pulpit, altar, and font were fashioned of rough-hewn wood. Yet was it sufficient for the wants of the age, and served the purpose of worship, the heart being rightly tuned, as the most gorgeous cathedral of after ages.

St. John had now resigned the Archbishopric
of York, and had retired to his monastery at
Beverlega, to spend the remnant of his life in
prayer, devotional exercises, and the seclusion of
the cloister. The Earl, a pious man, was on very
friendly terms with the ex-Archbishop, and
invited him to come and consecrate his church,
just finished, to which John readily assented, and,
despite his years and infirmities, on the appointed
day took up his walking staff and went on foot
through Westwood to South Burton, meditating
by the way on his past life, on his ancestral home
at Harpham-on-the-Wolds, his student's life
under St. Hilda at the Abbey of Streoneshalh,
his episcopal career at Hagulstadt, his
experience on the Archiepiscopal Throne of
York, and his retirement to the Abbey of Beverlega, acknowledging, with grateful thanksgiving,
the Providential hand that had sustained him
through his varied course of life. On the arrival
of the ex-Prelate at South Burton, he found the
family in great grief in consequence of the illness
of the Lady Puch, who had been stricken down
by a severe attack of fever, which threatened to
terminate her life. She was an exceedingly
devout woman, assiduous in her attention to the

duties of religion, charitable to the poor, and a great blessing to the poor and destitute of the village. A great portion of her time was spent in the educational training of her two lovely daughters, now approaching womanhood, and who much resembled her in the piety of their lives. She had now lain in bed a month, suffering agonies of torment, and expecting every day would be her last. Her husband wished to postpone the consecration of the church in consequence of her critical condition, but she would not listen to it. "Why," said she, "should the poor people be deprived of the privilege of hearing the service of God performed in a consecrated edifice because I, a poor insignificant mortal like themselves, am labouring under this affliction? Let the consecration take place the same as if I were well and able to take part in the ceremony; the thought of what is taking place will be more beneficial to me than all the doctor's medicine that shall be given me;" and it was determined that the ceremony should be proceeded with as if there were no impediment in the way.

Brithunus, a disciple of St. John, and the first abbot of his monastery, had also come over to assist in the ceremony, and to him we are

indebted for a narrative of the miracle which
accompanied it, as well as of many another
notable miracle performed by St. John, which he
communicated to Bede, who interwove them into
his Ecclesiastical History. The consecration was
duly performed according to the Anglo-Saxon
style, with singing, prayers, the sprinkling of
holy water, and a proclamation from the Archbishop that the edifice was now rendered sacred,
and become a temple of the Living God,
concluding with a benediction. "Then," says
Brithunus, "the Earl desired him to dine at his
house, but the Bishop declined, saying he must
return to the monastery. The Earl pressing him
more earnestly, vowed he would give alms to the
poor if the Bishop would break his fast that day
in his house. I joined my entreaties to his,
promising in like manner to give alms for the
relief of the poor if he would go and dine at the
Earl's house and give his blessing. Having at
length, with great difficulty, prevailed, we went
in to dine."

The banquet was served with the profusion
and splendour of the time, consisting chiefly
of boar's flesh, venison, fish, and birds, eaten from
platters of wood, with an ample supply of wine,

which was passed round in flagons of silver. In the course of the repast, the conversation was confined almost exclusively to two topics—the new church and the hopes that were entertained of its becoming a blessing to the neighbourhood, and the illness of the Earl's wife, with which the Bishop sympathised with much kindly feeling.

"Can nothing be done," inquired the Earl, "by means of the church to alleviate her sufferings, if not to restore her to health? The physicians are at their wit's end; they know nothing of the nature of the disease, and the remedies they give seem rather to aggravate than cure it. Peradventure the blessing of a holy man might have a beneficial effect."

"The issues of life and death," replied the Bishop, "are in the hands of God alone. Sometimes it is even impious to attempt to overrule His ordinations, which, although often inscrutable and productive of affliction and suffering, are intended for some ultimate good."

At this moment one of the lady's handmaidens entered the banqueting-room with a message from her mistress to the effect that her pains had materially lessened since the consecration had taken place, and that she desired a draught of the holy water that had been used, feeling an inward conviction that it, accompanied by the Bishop's blessing, would be of great service. "The Bishop then," continues Brithunus, "sent to the woman that lay sick some of the holy water which he had blessed for the consecration of the church, by one of the brothers that went along with me, ordering him to give her some to drink, and wash the place where her greatest pain was with some of the same. This being done, the woman immediately got up in health, and perceiving that she had not only been delivered from her tedious distemper, but at the same time recovered the strength which she had lost, she presented the cup to the Bishop and me, and continued serving us with drink, as she had begun, till dinner was over, following the example of Peter's mother-in-law, who, having been sick of a fever, arose at the touch of our Lord, and having at once received health and strength, ministered to them."

The two young daughters of the Earl, on witnessing the miraculous restoration to health of their beloved mother, had retired together to their chamber to offer up their heartfelt thanksgivings to God for her recovery, and before

the Bishop's departure came down to
the banqueting-hall and received his blessing.
They were exceedingly lovely both in form and
feature, and when they entered the hall, with
modest downcast eyes, it seemed to those present
as if two angelic beings from the celestial sphere
had deigned to visit them. "Come hither, my
children," said their mother, "and thank the good
Bishop for interceding with heaven on my behalf,
and who has thus been instrumental in delivering
me from the terrible disease under which I have
been labouring for so long a period." In response,
the young maidens went to the Bishop, and
kneeling at his feet, expressed their gratitude to
him for what he had done, and implored his
blessing. Placing his hands on their heads, he
said, "My dear daughters in Christ, attribute not
to me, a sinful mortal, that which is due alone to
our Merciful Father in Heaven, who has seen fit
first to afflict your mother with grievous trials
for some wise purpose, and then suddenly to
restore her to health, that her soul may be purified so as to enable her to pass through this lower
world, untainted by the grosser sins, but, like all
fallible mortals, to be still open to lesser temptations, that in the end she may be rendered meet

to enter that higher sphere of existence which is reserved for those who live holy lives here below. May God bless you, my dear daughters, tread in the footsteps of your saintly mother, that you also may be made meet for the same inheritance of light." So saying, the Bishop took up his staff, and bidding farewell to the Earl and his family, wended his way, accompanied by Brithunus and the monks, through Westwood to his home at Beverlega.

From this time the two young ladies continued to grow in stature and loveliness of person, as well as in fervent piety and the grace of God. They had sprung up into young womanhood, and many were the suitors for their hands who came fluttering about South Burton, knowing well that, as the Earl had no son, nor was likely to have one, they must, if they survived him, become his co-heiresses. But they refused to listen to the flatteries and protestations of everlasting love of these young fellows, not so much because they saw through the hollowness and feigned nature of their professions of love, but because they had determined to live lives of celibacy, devoted solely to the service of God. St. John made repeated visits to South Burton,

and nothing afforded them greater spiritual
comfort and holy pleasure than lengthened
converse with him on the things that pertain to
everlasting life. But a couple of years after the
consecration of the church he passed away to his
rest and reward, " with his memory overshadowed
by the benedictions of mankind," and was buried
in the portico of the church of Beverlega, which
he had founded.

A few years after this the two maidens, with
the full consent of their parents, entered the
convent of St. John, at Beverlega, to spend the
remainder of their lives in the holy seclusion of
the cloister. The Earl was an extensive landed
proprietor, with possessions in and about South
Burton, and others on the banks of the Hull,
near Grovehill, a landing-place of the Romans,
and now a suburb of Beverley, with some
extensive manufacturing works. When his
daughters entered the convent he bestowed upon
it the manor of Walkington, lying southward of
South Burton and abutting on Beverley Westwood. At the same time he made a grant to the
people of Beverlega of a tract of swampy land on
the banks of the Hull, to serve as a common
pasturage for their cattle. This tract of land,

now called Swinemoor, is still held by the burgesses of Beverley, forming one of the four valuable pastures, containing, in the aggregate, nearly 1,200 acres, the property of the freemen of the borough.

There are reasons for believing that a Christian Church existed on the shores of the Beaver Lake, in the wood of Deira, the site of the modern Beverley, in the time of the Ancient British Apostolic Christianity, which had formerly been the scene of the Druidical religion, which was destroyed by the pagan Saxons, and re-edified by St. John the Archbishop. In one of his progresses through his diocese, he came to this clearing in the wood of Deira, with its sacred beaver-lake, formerly called Llyn yr Avanc, now Inder-a-wood, and was struck by its sylvan beauty and its quiet seclusion. He found there a very small wooden church, thatched with reeds, which he determined to restore and enlarge, and founded, in connection with it, a religious house for both sexes—a monastery for men and a nunnery for women. He added to it a choir, and appointed seven priests to officiate at the altar; built the monastery, and endowed it with lands for its support. Hither he retired when enfeebled by age, and here he was buried in the porch of his church in the year 721.

It was to this nunnery that the Sisters Agnes and Agatha went, and after a period of probation, were despoiled of their hair, and assumed the veil of the sisterhood. The religious houses of the Saxons were not the luxurious abodes that they became in after years. The life led there was one of ascetic severity, with bare walls, hard pallets, scanty food of the simplest description, a continuous series of prayers and religious exercises, accompanied by frequent fastings, penances, and fleshly mortification, to all which the two sisters submitted with cheerfulness, as conducive to the spiritual health of their souls. They were never found sleeping when the summons for divine service was sounded forth, and they were ever willing to perform the most menial duties as tending to keep within them a spirit of Christian humility. Their profound piety and rigorous attention to disciplinary matters excited the admiration of the Mother Superior, but never would they lend ear to praises from her lips, lest it should engender spiritual pride, the aim of their lives being to rank as the lowest servants of the servants of

Christ. And thus the years passed along in one monotonous but ever-blessed sameness, ever dwelling within the walls and precincts of the nunnery, save on two occasions, when they went to South Burton to attend the funerals of their parents.

It was the eve of the Nativity, a bright starlight night, as that over Bethlehem when the three wise men of the East came thither guided by the wandering star. The nuns were assembled in their chapel for an early service, amongst whom were the two sisters apparently absorbed in divine meditation. The nuns then retired for their evening refection and silent contemplation in their cells until midnight, when the bell summoned them again to the chapel for midnight Mass, which was to usher in the holy day. At this service there was a strange and unwonted omission; the two sisters were absent. "Where are the Sisters Agnes and Agatha?" inquired the Abbess; "surely something has befallen them, else they would not be absent, especially on such an occasion as this. Go and search diligently for them." Every corner of the building and the grounds outside were searched, but in vain; not a vestige of them could be found; and at length,

L

as the hour of midnight was close at hand, the Mass was proceeded with. The following day, that of the Nativity, was devoted to the usual festal, religious duties; but a heaviness of heart pervaded the assembly, as the sisters had not re-appeared, and no tidings of them could be heard.

Days, weeks, and months passed away, and no clue to their mysterious disappearance presented itself until the eve of St. John, their patron saint. The vespers had been sung, with special reference to the coming day, and the nuns had gone out to breathe the air of the summer evening, whilst the Abbess, taking the key of the tower, unlocked the door and went up the stone stairs to the top, a place not much frequented, where she thought to offer up her prayers beneath the open dome of heaven, without any intervening walls. She had just placed her foot on the topmost stair when she was startled at beholding the two sisters lying locked in each other's arms and with upward turned eyes. At the first glance she supposed them to be dead, but a moment after was undeceived by their rising, and saying, "Mother, dear! it will soon be time for the midnight Mass; but how is this? We lay down an hour ago, under the sky of a winter night, but now we have awakened under the setting sun of a summer eve."

"An hour ago! my children," replied the Abbess, "it is now months since you disappeared on the eve of the Nativity, and months since the midnight Mass of the birth of our Saviour was sung. Can it be you have been sleeping here all through the interval?"

"Mother, dear," they replied, after some further questionings and explanations, "we have not been sleeping, we have been transported to heaven, and have seen sights inconceivable to the human eye, and heard music such as has never been listened to in this lower world. The heaven that we have visited is no mere localised spot, but extends throughout infinite space. It possesses no land or water; no mountains and valleys; no rivers, or lakes, or trees, or material objects of any kind; but has picturesque scenery, impalpable and cloudlike, of the most ravishing beauty. It is peopled by myriads of angelic beings and beatified mortals, unsubstantial and etherealised, all of exquisitely symmetrical figures, and with gloriously radiant features, beaming with happiness and smiling with serenity. Unlike the popular opinion, it is not a place of idle lounging and repose, but of intense activity, all being engaged in employments which afford an intensity of pleasurable emotions. The Almighty Father and Creator of all this realm of beauty and of all these glorified creatures it was not possible for us to see with our mortal eyes, but we were perfectly cognisant of his influence and presence everywhere throughout the infinitude of space. But oh! the music! here, on earth, it is termed divine, but our sweetest melodies are but a jarring discord of sounds compared with that of heaven; mortal ear cannot form the faintest conception of its sublime grandeur and unutterable loveliness."

Thus spake they to the astonished Abbess, who at once recognised the fact of their miraculous transportation to the realms of light for a temporary sojourn there, that on their return to earth they might be the means of comforting and encouraging those who by holy lives of asceticism, self-denial, and prayer, were wending their way thitherwards; and she conducted them down to their sister nuns, to whom again they had to narrate the visions that had been vouchsafed to them.

"There is joy in the convent of Beverley,
   Now these saintly maidens are found,
And to hear their story right wonderingly
   The nuns have gathered around ;
The long-lost maidens, to whom was given
   To live so long the life of heaven."

The Sisters further stated that the first spirit
they met was the holy St. John, the founder of
their convent, whom they immediately recognised,
although he had cast off his earthly integuments,
and appeared in a glorified form, but in semblance
as when he performed the miracle at South
Burton.

He welcomed them with affectionate warmth,
and told them that their parents were now
enjoying the reward of their virtuous and
pious lives, but that they could not be permitted
to see them until they themselves had finally
passed away from earthly life. He further told
them that he kept a watchful eye over his town
and monastery in Inderawood, with affectionate
love, which should be seen in after ages, in the
promotion of their prosperity.

The next day the festival of St. John was
celebrated in the monastery and church, with
more than usual interest and devotion. Towards
the close of it—

"The maidens have risen, with noiseless tread
    They glide o'er the marble floor ;
They seek the Abbess with bended head :
    'Thy blessing we would implore,
Dear mother ! for e'er the coming day
    Shall blush into light, we must hence away.'
The Abbess hath lifted her gentle hands,
    And the words of peace hath said,
'O vade in pacem ;' aghast she stands,
    'Have their innocent spirits fled ?'
Yes, side by side lie these maidens fair,
    Like two wreaths of snow in the moonlight there."

At the same time the church became lighted up
with a supernatural roseate hue, and sounds of
celestial music ravished the ears of the assembly.
The Sisters were laid side by side by tender and
reverent hands in a tomb near the altar of the
church, and now—

"Fifty summers have come and passed away,
    But their loveliness knoweth no decay ;
And many a chaplet of flowers is hung,
    And many a bead told there ;
And many a hymn of praise is sung,
    And many a low-breathed prayer ;
And many a pilgrim bends the knee
    At the shrine of the Sisters of Beverley."

The tomb of the Sisters was destroyed in the
great fire of 1188, which destroyed not only St.
John's Church and monastery, but the whole

town besides. They were afterwards rebuilt —
the Minster in the superb style which it now
presents — and it was in remembrance of these
sainted Sisters that the uninscribed tomb was
placed in the new church.

This legend has formed the subject of an
exquisite poem, which appeared in the pages of
the *Literary Gazette*, and has been attributed to
the pen of Alaric A. Watts, which, however, is
open to doubt.

The Dragon of Wantley.

NCE on a time—as the old story-tellers were wont to commence their tales of love, chivalry, and romance— there dwelt in the most wild and rugged part of Wharncliffe Chase, near Rotherham, a fearful dragon, with iron teeth and claws. How he came there no one knew, or where he came from ; but he proved to be a most pestilent neighbour to the villagers of Wortley—blighting the crops by the poisonous stench of his breath, devouring the cattle of the fields, making no scruple of seizing upon a plump child or a tender young virgin to serve as a *bonne-bouche* for his breakfast table, and even crunching up houses and churches to satisfy his ravenous appetite.

Wortley, is situated in the parish of Penistone, and belongs now, as it has done for centuries, to the Wortley family. Before the dissolution of monasteries, the Rectory of Penistone belonged to the Abbey of St.

Stephen, Westminster, and was granted, when the Abbey was dissolved, to Thomas Howard, third Duke of Norfolk, who out of the proceeds established in Sheffield a set of almshouses. The impropriation of the great tithes were let to the Wortley family, who, by measures of oppression and extortion, contrived to get a great deal more than they were entitled to, and Nicholas Wortley insisted on taking the tithes in kind, but was opposed by Francis Bosville, who obtained a decree (17th Elizabeth) against him; but Sir Francis Wortley, in the succeeding reign, again attempted to enforce payment in kind, with so much disregard to the suffering he inflicted upon the poor that they determined upon finding out some champion who would dare to attack this redoubtable dragon in his den at Wantley, so as to put an end, once and for all, to the destruction of their crops, the loss of their cattle, and the desolation of their ruined homes. Foremost in this movement was one Lyonel Rowlestone, who married the widow of Francis Bosville; and the parishioners entered into an agreement to unite in opposition to the claims of the Wortleys. The parchment on which it is written is dated 1st James I., and bristles with

the names and seals of the people of Penistone of
of that time, and is still extant.

In the neighbourhood, on a moor not far from
Bradfield, stood a mansion called More or Moor
Hall, and was inhabited by a family who had
resided there from the time of Henry II., but of
whom little is known, excepting the wonderful
achievement of one member of the family,
" More of More Hall," who slew the Dragon of
Wantley.

The family had for their crest a green
dragon, and there was formerly in Bradfield
Church a stone dragon, five feet in length, which
had some connection with the family.   To this
worthy, who, it is supposed, may have been an
attorney or counsellor, the parishioners of Penistone, having decided upon appealing to the law
courts, applied to undertake their case, and make
battle on the terrible dragon in his den among
the rocks of the forest of Wharncliffe.   He
readily complied with their wish, and with great
boldness and valour prepared for the conflict by
going to Sheffield and ordering a suit of armour,
studded with spikes—that is, arming himself with
the panoply of law, and then went forth and
made the attack.   The fight is said, in the

ballad narrative, to have lasted two days and nights, probably the duration of the lawsuit, and in the end he killed the dragon, or won his suit, thus relieving the people of Penistone from any further annoyance or unjust exaction from that quarter. Sir Francis Wortley persuaded his cousin Wordsworth, the freehold lord of the manor (ancestor, lineal or collateral, of the Poet Wordsworth), to stand aloof in the matter, and now the Wortley and the Wordsworth are the only estates in the parish that pay tithes.

To commemorate the event an exceedingly humorous and cleverly satirical ballad was written, which, being also a lively burlesque on the ballad romances of chivalry, served the same purpose towards them that Cervantes' "Don Quixote" did for the prose fictions of the same character. Thus opens the ballad—

"Old stories tell how Hercules
　A dragon slew at Gerna,
With seven heads and fourteen eyes
　To see and well discerna ;
But he had a club, this dragon to drub,
　Or he had ne'er I warrant ye ;
But More of More Hall with nothing at all,
　He slew the dragon of Wantley.

> " This dragon had two furious wings,
> 　　Each one upon each shoulder :
> With a sting in his tail, as long as a flail,
> 　　Which made him bolder and bolder.
> He had long claws, and in his jaws
> 　　Four and forty teeth of iron ;
> With a hide as tough as any buff,
> 　　Which did him round environ."

It then goes on to describe how " he ate three children at one sup, as one would eat an apple." Also all sorts of cattle and trees, the forest beginning to diminish very perceptibly, and " houses and churches," which to him were geese and turkeys, " leaving none behind."

> " But some stones, dear Jack, that he could not crack,
> 　　Which on the hills you will finda."

These stones are supposed to be a reference to the Lyonel Rowlestone, who was the leader of the opposition. There are many local allusions of a similar character, which would no doubt add much to the keenness of the satire and the humour, but which are lost to us through our ignorance of the circumstances and persons alluded to.

" In Yorkshire, near fair Rotherham," was his den, and at Wantley a well from which he drank.

"Some say this dragon was a witch,
  Some say he was a devil;
For from his nose a smoke arose
  And with it burning snivel."

" Hard by a furious knight there dwelt," who
could " wrestle, play at quarter-staff, kick, cuff,
and huff; and with his hands twain could swing
a horse till he was dead, and eat him all up but
his head." To this wonderful athlete came
" men, women, girls, and boys, sighing and
sobbing, and made a hideous noise—O! save us
all, More of More Hall, thou peerless knight of
these woods; do but slay this dragon, who won't
leave us a rag on, we'll give thee all our goods."
The Knight replied—

"Tut, tut," quoth he, "no goods I want;
  But I want, I want, in sooth,
A fair maid of sixteen, that's brisk and keen,
  With smiles about her mouth;
Hair black as sloe, skin white as snow,
  With blushes her cheeks adorning;
To anoint me o'er night, e'er I go to the fight,
  And to dress me in the morning."

This being agreed to, he hied to Sheffield, and
had a suit of armour, covered with spikes five or
six inches long, made, which, when he donned it,
caused the people to take him for " an Egyptian
porcupig," and the cattle for " some strange,

outlandish hedgehog." When he rose in the
morning,

> "To make him strong and mighty
> He drank, by the tale, six pots of ale
> And a quart of *aqua vitæ*."

Thus equipped and with his valour braced up,
he went to Wantley, concealing himself in the
well, and when the dragon came to drink, he
shouted "Boh," and struck the monster a blow
on the mouth. The knight then came out of the
well, and they commenced fighting, for some time
without advantage on either side—without either
receiving a wound. At length, however, after
fighting two days and a night, the dragon gave
him a blow which made him reel and the earth to
quake. "But More of More Hall, like a valiant
son of Mars," returned the compliment with such
vigour that—

> "Oh! quoth the dragon, with a deep sigh,
>   And turned six times together;
>   Sobbing and tearing, cursing and swearing
>   Out of his throat of leather;
>   More of More Hall! O, thou rascal!
>   Would I had seen thee never;
>   With the thing on thy foot, thou has pricked my gut
>   And I'm quite undone for ever.

" Murder ! murder ! the dragon cry'd.
　　Alack ! alack ! for grief ;
　Had you but mist that place, you could
　　Have done me no mischief.
　Then his head he shaked, trembled and quaked,
　　And down he laid and cry'd,
　First on one knee, then on back tumbled he :
　　So groan'd, kick't, and dy'd."

Henry Carey, in 1738, brought out an opera on the subject, entitled " The Dragon of Wantley," abounding in humour, and a fine burlesque on the Italian operas of the period, then the rage of fashion. And in 1873, Poynter exhibited at the Royal Academy a picture of " More of More Hall and the Dragon."

The Miracles and Ghost of Watton.

IN a sweetly sequestered spot, environed by patriarchal trees of luxuriant foliage, between the towns of Driffield and Beverley, nestles a Tudoresque building, which goes by the name of Watton Abbey, although it never was an abbey, but a Gilbertine Priory. It is now a private residence, and was occupied for many years as a school, the existing buildings apparently having been erected since the dissolution, and there are but few remains of the original convent, saving a portion of the nunnery, now converted into stables, a hollow square indicating the site of the kitchen and the moat which originally surrounded the entire enclosure. A couple of centuries ago there were extensive remains of the old priory, but they were removed for the purpose of repairing Beverley Minster. Moreover, the abbey has a haunted room, which, however, has no connection with the monastic times, although the ghost that haunts it is usually designated "The Headless Nun of Watton," but belongs to the civil war period of the seventeenth century. The fact is that story tellers of the legend confound two altogether different narratives—the one of a trangressing nun of the twelfth century, and the other of a murdered lady of the seventeenth, combining their two histories into one story, as if their persons were identical.

A nunnery was established here in a very early period of Anglo-Saxon Christianity, probably soon after its re-introduction into Northumbria by King Oswald, as we find St. John of Beverley performing a miracle there, which would be about the year 720, after he had resigned his Bishopric and retired to Beverley. It appears that he was an intimate friend of the Lady Prioress—Heribury—and made frequent visits to Watton to administer spiritual advice and ghostly consolation to the inmates under her charge. On one occasion when he went thither, he found the Prioress's daughter suffering great agony from a diseased and swollen arm, the result of unskilful bleeding, and was solicited to go to her chamber and give her his blessing, which might be the means of alleviating the pain.

M

He inquired when she had been bled, and was told on the fourth day of the moon, which he said was a very inauspicious day, quoting Archbishop Theodore as his authority, and he feared his prayers would be of no avail. Nevertheless he went to her room, prayed for her restoration to health, gave her his blessing, and went down to dinner. They had, however, scarcely seated themselves when a servant came in, stating that all her pain had gone, her swollen arm had been reduced to its natural size, and that she was perfectly restored to health, and was dressing to come down and dine with them.

The nunnery was destroyed, it is presumed, by the Danes at the same time that the Monastery of Beverley perished at their hands, in the ninth century, and it lay waste and desolate until the twelfth century, although we find from the Domesday survey that there were then a church and priest in the village.

In 1148-9, Eustace Fitz John, Lord of Knaresborough, and a favourite of King Henry I., at the instance of Murdac, Archbishop of York, refounded the convent, in atonement for certain crimes he had committed. It was established for thirteen canons and thirty-six nuns of the new Gilbertine order, who were to live in the same block of buildings, but with a party wall for the separation of the sexes; the canons "to serve the nuns perpetually in terrene as well as in divine matters." He endowed it with the Lordship of Watton, with all its appurtenances in pure and perpetual alms for the salvation of his soul, and those of his wife, his father and mother, brothers and sisters, friends and servants.

Archbishop Murdac was at the time resident at Beverley, the gates of York having been shut against him; and it may be that the fact of his predecessor, St. John, the patron-saint of the town where he dwelt, having performed a great miracle there, was what influenced him in his desire to see a resuscitation of the monastery. He was a remarkable man, and had led a somewhat adventurous life. Archbishop Thurstan was his patron, and gave him some preferments in the church of York, which he resigned at the pressing invitation of St. Bernard, founder of the Cistercians, to become a monk at Clervaux. Soon after he was sent by his superior to found a Cistercian house at Vauclair, of which he was appointed the first abbot, in 1131, where he remained until 1143, when, at the recommendation of St. Bernard, he was elected Abbot of Fountains. Under his judicious and able government the abbey prospered and threw off not less than seven offshoots—those of Kirkstall, Lix, Meaux, Vaudy, and Woburn.

On the death of Archbishop Thurstan, King Stephen desired the canons to elect William Fitzherbert, his nephew and their treasurer, in his place, which they were willing to do, but the Cistercians, headed by Murdac, suspecting that undue influence had been made use of, vehemently opposed his election, and Pope Eugenius, on the appeal of St. Bernard, suspended Fitzherbert.

Fitzherbert, out of revenge, went with his friends to Fountains, broke open the door, searched ineffectually for Murdac, then fired the abbey, and retired. This act caused a great sensation, and the Archbishop was deprived in 1147. The same year an assembly met at Richmond, and elected Murdac as Archbishop, who immediately went to Rome and obtained his pall from Pope Eugenius; but on his return found York barred against his entrance, upon which he retired to Beverley. Stephen, the King, refused to recognise him, sequestering the stalls of York, and fining the town of Beverley for harbouring him. It was at this time that he promoted the re-establishment of Watton, and placed within its walls a child of four years of age to be educated, with a view of taking the veil.

In retaliation, he excommunicated Puisnet, Treasurer of York, and laid the city under an interdict. Puisnet was afterwards elected Bishop of Durham, upon which Murdac excommunicated the Prior and Archdeacon, who came to Beverley to implore pardon, and could only obtain absolution on acknowledging their fault and submitting to scourging at the entrance to Beverley Minster. He died at Beverley in the same year (1153), and was buried in York Cathedral.

Elfleda, the child whom Murdac had placed in the convent, was a merry, vivacious little creature; and whilst but a child was a source of amusement to the sisterhood, who, although prim and demure in bearing, and some of them sour-tempered and acid in their tempers, were wont to smile at her youthful frolics and ringing laugh; but as she grew older, her outbursts of merriment, and the sallies of wit that began to animate her conversation, were checked, as being inconsistent with the character of a young lady who was now enrolled as novice, preparatory to taking the veil. As she advanced towards womanhood her form gradually developed into a most symmetrical figure; and her features became the perfection of beauty, set off with a transparent delicacy of complexion, such as would have rendered her a centre of attraction even among the beauties of a Royal Court. This excited the jealousy of the sisters, who were chiefly elderly and middle-aged spinsters, whose homely and somewhat coarse features had proved detrimental to their hopes of obtaining husbands. They began to treat her with scornful looks, chilling neglect, and petty persecutions; but when she, later on, evinced a manifest repugnance to convent life, ridiculed the ways of the holy sisters, and even satirised them, they charged her with entertaining rebellious and ungodly sentiments, and subjected her to penances and other modes of wholesome correction, such as they considered would subdue her worldly spirit.

Sprightly and light-hearted as she was, Elfleda was not happy, immured as she was within these detested walls, and condemned to assist in wearisome services, such as she thought might perhaps be congenial to the souls of her elder sisters, whose hopes of worldly happiness and conjugal endearment had been blighted, but which were altogether unsuited for one so beautiful (for she knew that she was fair, and was vain of her looks) and so cheerful-minded as herself; and she longed with intense desire to make her escape, mingle with the outer world, and have free intercourse with the other sex.

According to the charter of endowment, the lay brethren of the monastery were entrusted with the management of the secular affairs of the nunnery, which necessitated their admission within its portals on certain occasions for conference with the prioress. On these occasions Elfleda would cast furtive and very un-nunlike glances upon their persons. She was particularly attracted by one of them, a young man of prepossessing mien and seductive style of speech, and she felt her heart beat wildly whenever he came with the other visitors. He noticed her surreptitious glances, and saw that she was exceedingly beautiful, and his heart responded to the sentiment he felt that he had inspired in hers. They maintained this silent but eloquent

language of love for some time, and soon found
means of having stolen interviews under the
darkness of night, when vows of everlasting love
were interchanged, and led, eventually, to
consequences which at the outset were not
dreamt of by the erring pair.

Suspicion having been excited by her altered
form, she was summoned before her superiors on
a charge of "transgressing the conventual rules
and violating one of the most stringent laws of
monastic life," and as concealment was impossible,
she boldly confessed her fault, adding that she
had no vocation for a convent life, and desired to
be banished from the community. This request
could not be listened to for a moment. The
culprit had brought a scandal and indelible stain
upon the fair fame of the house, which must, at
any cost, be concealed from the world; and her
open avowal of her guilt raised in the breasts of
the pious sisterhood a perfect fury of indignation,
and a determination to inflict immediate and
condign punishment on her. It was variously
suggested that she should be burnt to death, that
she should be walled up alive, that she should be
flayed, that her flesh should be torn from her
bones with red-hot pincers, that she should be

roasted to death before a fire, etc. ; but the more prudent and aged averted these extreme measures, and suggested some milder forms of punishment, which were at once carried out. The miserable object of their vengeance was stripped of her clothing, stretched on the floor, and scourged with rods until the blood trickled down profusely from her lacerated back. She was then cast into a noisome dungeon, without light, fettered by iron chains to the floor, and supplied with only bread and water, "which was administered with bitter taunts and reproaches."

Meanwhile the young man, her paramour, had left the monastery, and as the nuns were desirous of inflicting some terrible punishment upon him for his horrible crime, they extorted from Elfleda, under promise that she should be released and given up to him, the confession that he was still in the neighbourhood in disguise, and that not knowing of the discovery that had been made, he would come to visit her, and make the usual signal of throwing a stone on the roof over her sleeping cell. The Prioress made this known to the brethren of the monastery, and arranged with them for his capture. The following night he came, looked cautiously round, and then threw the stone, when the monks rushed out of ambush, cudgelled him soundly, and then took him a prisoner into the house. "The younger part of the nuns, inflamed with a pious zeal, demanded the custody of the prisoner, on pretence of gaining further information. Their request was granted, and taking him to an unfrequented part of the convent, they committed on his person such brutal atrocities as cannot be translated without polluting the page on which they are written; and, to increase the horror, the lady was brought forth to be witness of the abominable scene." Whilst lying in her dungeon, Elfleda became penitent, and conscious of having committed a gross crime, and one night whilst sleeping in her fetters, Archbishop Murdac appeared to her and charged her with having cursed him. She replied that she certainly had cursed him for having placed her in so uncongenial a sphere. "Rather curse yourself," said he, "for having given way to temptation." "So I do," she answered, "and I regret having imputed the blame to you." He then exhorted her to repentance and the daily repetition of certain psalms, and then vanished,—a vision which afforded her much consolation.

The holy sisters were now much troubled on the question of what should be done with the infant which was expected daily, and preparations were made for its reception; when Elfleda was again visited by the Archbishop, accompanied by two women who, " with the holy aid of the Archbishop, safely delivered her of the infant, which they bore away in their arms, covered with a fair linen cloth." When the nuns came the next morning they found her in perfect health and restored to her youthful appearance, without any signs of the accouchement, and charged her with murdering the infant,—a very improbable idea, seeing that she was still chained to the floor. She narrated what had occurred, but was not believed. The next night all her fetters were miraculously removed, and when her cell was entered the following morning she was found standing free, and the chains not to be found.

The Father Superior of the convent was then called in, and he invited Alured, Abbot of Rievaulx, to assist him in the investigation of the case, who decided that it was a miraculous intervention, and the Abbot departed, saying, " What God hath cleansed call not thou common or unclean, and whom He hath loosed thou mayest not bind."

What afterwards became of Elfleda is not stated, but we may presume that after these miraculous events she would be admitted as a thrice holy member of the sisterhood, despite her little peccadillo.

Alured of Rievaulx, the monkish chronicler, narrates the substance of the above circumstances, and vouches for their truth. "Let no one," says he, "doubt the truth of this account, for I was an eye-witness to many of the facts, and the remainder were related to me by persons of such mature age and distinguished piety, that I cannot doubt the accuracy of the statement."

This is the story of the frail and unfortunate nun; the other, which is usually dovetailed on the former, is of much more recent date. In the present house there is a chamber wainscoted throughout with panelled oak, one of the panels forming a door, so accurately fitted that it cannot be distinguished from the other panels. It is opened by a secret spring, and communicates with a stone stair that goes down to the moat; it may be that the room was a hiding-place for the Jesuits or priests of the Catholic Church when they were so ruthlessly hunted down and barbarously executed in the Elizabethan and Jacobean reigns. The room is reputed to be haunted by the ghost of a headless lady with an infant in her arms, who comes, or came thither formerly, to sleep nightly, the bed-clothes being found the following morning in a disordered state, as they would be after a person had been sleeping in them. If by chance any person had daring enough to occupy the room, the ghost would come, minus the head, dressed in blood-stained garments, with her infant in her arms, and would stand motionless at the foot of the bed for a while, and then vanish. A visitor on one occasion, who knew nothing of the legend, was put to sleep in the chamber, who in the morning stated that his slumbers had been disturbed by a spectral visitant, in the form of a lady with bloody raiment and an infant, and that her features bore a strange resemblance to those of a lady whose portrait hung in the room; from which it would appear that on that special occasion she had donned her head.

According to the legend, a lady of distinction who then occupied the house was a devoted Royalist in the great civil war which resulted in the death of King Charles. It was after the battle of Marston Moor, which was a death-blow to the Royalists north of the Humber, and when the Parliamentarians dominated the broad lands of Yorkshire, that a party of fanatical Round-heads came into the neighbourhood of Watton, " breathing out threatenings and slaughter " against the " malignants," and especially against such as still clung to the " vile rags of the whore of Babylon," vowing to put all such to the sword. The Lady of Watton, who was a devout Catholic, heard of this band of Puritan soldiers, who were " rampaging " over the Wolds, and of the barbarous murders of which they had been guilty. Her husband was away fighting in the ranks of the King down Oxford way, and she was left without any protector excepting a handful of servants, male and female, who would be of no use against a band of armed soldiers, and it was with great fear and trembling that she heard of their arrival at Driffield, some three or four miles distant, where they had been plundering and maltreating " the Philistines ; " fearing more for her infant than herself, as she believed the prevalent exaggerated rumour, that it was a favourite amusement with them to toss babies up in the air and catch them on the points of their pikes.

At length news was brought that the marauders were on the march to Watton, for the purpose of plundering it, as the home of a malignant, and the lady, for better security, shut herself, with her child and her jewels, in the wainscoted room, hoping in case of extremity to escape by means of a secret stair, and in the meanwhile committed herself and child to the care of the Virgin Mother. It was not long ere the band of soldiers arrived and hammered at the door, calling aloud for admittance, but met with no response. They were about breaking down the door, and went in search of implements for the purpose, when they caught sight of a low archway opening upon the moat, which they guessed to be a side entrance to the house, and crossing the moat, they found the stair, which they ascended and came to the panel, which they concluded was a disguised door. A few blows sufficed to dash it open, and they came into the presence of the lady, who was prostrate before a crucifix. Rising up, she demanded what they wanted, and wherefore this rude intrusion. They replied that they had come to despoil the

"Egyptian" who owned the mansion, and if he had been present, to smite him to death as a worshipper of idols and an abomination in the eyes of God.

An angry altercation ensued, the lady, who possessed a high spirit, making a free use of her tongue in upbraidings and reproaches for their dastardly conduct on the Wolds, of which she had heard, to which they listened very impatiently, and replied in coarse language not fit for a lady's ears, at the same time demanding the plate and other valuables of the house. She scornfully refused to give them up, and told them that if they wanted them they must find them for themselves, and at length so provoked them by her taunts that they cried, "Hew down with the sword the woman of Belial and the spawn of the malignant," and suiting the action to the word, they caught her child from her arms, dashed its brains out against the wall, and then cut her down and "hewed" off her head, after which they plundered the house and departed with their spoil.

It must not be supposed that these ruffians were a fair specimen of the brave, God-fearing men who fought under Fairfax, and put New-

castle and Rupert to flight at Marston Moor, who
fought with the sword in one hand and the Bible
in the other, who laid the axe at the root of
Royal abitrary prerogative, and were the real
authors of the civil and religious liberty which we
now enjoy. But, as in all times of civil com-
motion, there were evil-minded wretches who,
for purpose of plunder, assumed the garb and
adopted the phraseology of the noble-minded
soldiers of Fairfax and Hampden, and the Iron-
sides of Cromwell, out-Puritaned them in their
hypocritical cant, bringing disgrace and scandal
upon the armies with which they associated
themselves. And such were the villains who despoiled Watton, and slew so barbarously the poor
lady and her infant; and from that time the ghost
of the lady has haunted the room in which the
deed was perpetrated.

In the year 1780, Mr. Bethell, the then
occupier of the house, was giving a dinner-party
in the dining-room, which adjoined the haunted
apartment. When they were seated over their
wine the host related the story of the ghost, and
had scarcely finished it when an unearthly sound
issued from the floor beneath their feet. Consternation seized on the party. They concluded

N

that it was the ghost, and to their imagination the candles began to emit a blue, ghostly light. It seemed to be a confirmation of the truth of the story; but they summoned up courage enough to make an examination, and although it was approaching the " witching hour of night," they sent for a carpenter, who took up some planks of the floor, and found—not the ghost, but the nest of an otter from the moat, who had made there a home for her progeny, whose cries had alarmed them; and thus was dissipated what might otherwise have been deemed a veritable supernatural visitation.

The Murdered Hermit of Eskdale.

SIR Richard de Veron was a distinguished knight of the North Riding, who held a considerable estate by knight's service of the De Brus family in Cleveland. He was one of the heroes of the Battle of the Standard, in 1138, who went forth at the behest of Archbishop Thurstan to oppose the invasion of David of Scotland, and who signally defeated that monarch. A few years after, he joined the forces of the Empress Maud, whose pretensions to the throne of England he considered to be more legitimate than those of Stephen, and fought on her side at Lincoln, in 1141, when the King was defeated and taken prisoner, continuing to uphold her cause until she was compelled to retire from England. The war being thus brought to an end, and the adherents of the Empress generally declining to take service under a King whom they deemed a usurper, and by whom they were looked upon with suspicion, De

Veron sheathed his sword and retired to his family and home in Cleveland. He had a wife, whom he dearly loved, and two children, a boy—his heir, and a sweet little daughter for whom he entertained the most tender affection; indeed, although he delighted in the clash of arms and the exciting revelry of war, he was never so truly happy as when in the midst of his family, teaching his young son to ride, practice at the target, and follow his hounds in pursuit of the wild animals of the chase; or listening to the prattle of his little daughter, when taking lessons from her mother in reading, music, or embroidery work. Thus happily passed a few months after his return from his martial pursuits, when one morning, news was brought that a case of plague had occurred in the village, causing, as it always did, great consternation not only amongst the villagers, but in the knight's mansion, which stood half a mile away from the village. It was hoped that it might be an isolated case, and such rude remedial measures as were then known were adopted to prevent the spread of the infection, but within a week another case was reported, and another and another in rapid succession, after which it spread with fearful speed, until half the population succumbed to it, and were hastily buried without the usual funeral rites. In a month the disease appeared to be dying out, the deaths were fewer and fewer day by day, and it was fondly hoped that the terrible infliction was passing away, but it was not until three-fourths of the people had fallen victims to its pestilential fury.

Although Sir Richard hesitated not to go down to the village and employ himself in administering food, medicine, and consolation to the afflicted, he took every known precaution against coming into too close contact with the infected; he kept his family closely shut up at home, and occupied a separate set of apartments himself, not allowing them to come into his presence; but notwithstanding all his preventive measures he was at last stricken down. He gave positive orders that he should be left alone, and if it was God's will that he should die, he declared his resolution that he would die alone, and with affectionate earnestness sent a message to his wife, entreating her to remain apart from him, and not imperil her dear life by coming to his bedside. But she, true wife as she was, heeded not the risk to her own life, so long as she could afford comfort and spiritual consolation to him, in what might very probably be his last few moments on earth, and regardless of the injunction, hastened, on receiving the message, to the room where he lay. He reproached her gently for exposing herself to the risk of infection, but was met by assurances that it was not possible for her to remain away whilst he was lying there requiring careful tendence, with all the servants standing aloof panic-stricken, or flying from the house. He implored her to retire, but she replied that she might or might not take the infection; that was as God pleased, and if she did she might or might not fall a victim, but most assuredly if she left him alone and shut herself up away from him she would die of anxiety, or, in case of his death, of a broken heart. Finding remonstrance useless, he was fain to submit to her nursing, and happily during the night the malady passed its crisis, his strong, healthy constitution enabling him to battle successfully with the disease, and he gradually became convalescent.

Happiness again seemed to be dawning over the household, but it was not destined to last long. The faithful wife, who had watched so tenderly over his sick bed, regardless of the risk she ran, maintained her health so long as her services were needed, but in her ministrations she had imbibed the seed of the fatal malady, and now, when her husband was restored to health, the terrible plague spot made its appearance, and so rapidly did the disease develop itself that, within twenty-four hours, she fell a victim to its remorseless energy. It was a fearful blow to Sir Richard, but this was not all the suffering he had to undergo. Scarcely had he returned from the obsequies of his wife, when his two children caught the infection, and in another four-and-twenty hours they were both carried off, leaving him bereft of all the best-beloved of his soul, and sunk in the depths of desolation and despair.

For some months he remained in his silent and cheerless home in a state of profound apathy, taking no interest in the avocations devolving on him as the lord of an extensive estate. It is true he befriended, pecuniarily, the numerous widows and orphans left in the village by the ruthless pestilence that had swept over it, and he contributed large sums of money to the Church for prayers and masses for the souls of the departed, not only of his own family, but of his

vassals and dependants.   Nothing seemed capable
of rousing him from the despondency into which
he had fallen; the sports of the field were
altogether neglected; the cheerful companionship
of friends presented no attractions for him, and he
sat at home hour after hour through the live-long
day, plunged in moody melancholy and repining
meditation on his irreparable loss, and the utter
extinction of all that was worth living for.   And
thus passed week after week and month after
month, Time, the great mollifier of grief, seeming
to impart no balm to his sorrow-stricken soul.

The only person whom he admitted as a visitor,
besides those who came on imperative business
matters, was Father Anselm, a pious and devout
man, the priest of the village church.   It was in
his company only, and in listening to his spiritual
converse, that he felt any relief from the grief
that oppressed him, and gradually, after many
interviews, he began to look upon his affliction as
a providential dispensation, intended for some
wise purpose.   Gradually also he became more
weaned from earthly and secular things, and his
soul to become more spiritualised, and he began
to experience a feeling of attraction to the cloister.
One day he mentioned this to his spiritual

adviser, and Father Anselm, rejoicing thereat, warmly applauded the feeling, urging that such self-devotion would be most acceptable to God, and that it was only in religious meditation and prayer that he would be vouchsafed that true consolation which religion alone could give. The holy father perhaps was not altogether single-minded in thus fostering the idea of assuming the cowl, for he was a true Churchman, considering that the promotion of the temporal aggrandise-ment of the Church was an essential part of the duty of a Christian, a sentiment then universally prevalent, and not unusual now. He knew that Sir Richard was the owner of broad acres, and that now he had no heir to inherit them, and he often made delicate and incidental allusions to the fact, which seemed to produce an impression on the mind of the knight. At last an opportunity offered itself of speaking out more openly. With a profound sigh, Sir Richard one day said, when the conversation had turned upon his estates and possessions, "Alas! why should I trouble or concern myself about these lands and the improvements that might be made on them? I shall never more be able to derive pleasure from the possession of them, and I have no heir to bequeath them to. What is the good of riches if they do not afford happiness? A crust and water from the wayside brook with happiness is better than untold wealth accompanied with sorrow and anguish of heart."

Father Anselm saw his opportunity, and pertinently asked, " Since you have no heir, why not make the holy Church of Christ your heir? By doing so you would garner up for yourself riches in heaven—an eternity of inconceivable happiness compared with which in duration your present suffering is but as the pang of a moment."

Sir Richard sat musing for the space of a quarter of an hour, and then said, " Holy Father, what you say seems good, fitting, and worthy of consideration. Give me a week to think it over, and at the expiration of that period I will commune with you further on the subject," and Father Anselm took his departure.

At the week's end, when they met again, Sir Richard opened the subject by saying, "Venerable Father, I have since our last meeting given deep consideration to your counsels, and have come to the resolution of doing as you advise me. I have determined on assuming the monkish habit;

spending the remainder of my life in pious communion with some holy brotherhood; and on resigning my possessions into the hands of the Church of God."

"It is good," replied Father Anselm. "Have you thought of any specific house on which to bestow your donation?"

"It occurred to me," continued Sir Richard, "to become a canon of the Augustinian house recently founded by my feudal Lord, Robert de Brus, at Guisborough, and to add my lands to its further endowment."

"Permit me to counsel you otherwise," said the Father, "Guisborough, as an Augustinian house, is not so strict in its discipline as other monastic houses, and is already very fairly endowed. But there is another, of the Benedictine order, where you would have an opportunity of cultivating a more strictly religious and less secular frame of mind—I mean Whitby, a holy spot, once sanctified by the presence of the blessed St. Hilda. It was founded by King Oswy in 687, was laid in ruins by the sacrilegious Danes in 867, and so remained for another couple of hundred years, when God moved the heart of Will de Percy to refound it as a Priory. Within the last few years it has again been converted into an Abbey ; but it lacks endowment for the due maintenance of its superior dignity.   Let me advise you, therefore, to cast in your lot with these Benedictines, and win the approval of God by bestowing your wealth in his service, where it is much needed."

Sir Richard assented to this suggestion, caused a deed of gift to be drawn, in which he conveyed his lands to the Abbot and convent of Whitby, and entered the house as a novice ; and in due time, at the expiration of his novitiate, was admitted as a monk.

Brother Jerome (to use his monastic appellation) soon attracted notice by the fervour of his piety, his asceticism, and a strict and sincere observance of the conventual rules ; as well as by his humility and obedience to the ordinances of his superiors.   It chanced that after he had been in the house a few years, the Prior, whose position was that of sub-Abbot in the house, sickened and died ; and, at a meeting of the chapter to elect his successor, Brother Jerome was suggested as the most fitting, by his manifest piety and abilities, for the office ; but he resolutely declined taking it upon himself, preferring, as he said, to be rather a hewer of wood or drawer of water—the servant of the brotherhood—than to hold any superior office.

In the course of his meditations he was wont to cast a retrospective glance on his past life, and to grieve over his career as a soldier and a shedder of blood; especially did he mourn over the excesses of barbarous cruelty into which he had been drawn in emulation of the ferocity of his fellow-soldiers, when marching under the banner of the Empress, remembering with tears of bitter remorse, the burning villages, the homeless people, the corpse-strewn fields, and the widows and orphans they left in their rear. The more he thought of these past phases of his life, the more intense became his self-reproaches and the compunction excited by a sense of guilt and sin. He sought by mortification and maceration of the flesh to make atonement for these blood-stained deeds, but despite these self-inflicted punishments, he was not able to find rest for his soul. For ever, when prostrate in prayer, would they rise up before him, and the enemy of mankind would whisper in his ear, " Thou fool! what is the good of praying and fasting and weeping ? Thy sins are too heinous for pardon;

thou hast given up thy possessions to secure a
heritage in heaven, but thy guilt is so damning
that thou wilt assuredly find its gate shut against
thee.   Instead of leading a miserable and wretched
life here in the cloister, return to the world and
enjoy life while it lasts, for in either case there is
nothing to hope for in the future."

Jerome took counsel of the Abbot, an old,
wise, and experienced Christian, who at once
detected the cloven hoof in the temptation, and
was successful in convincing the tempted one of
the fact, advising him to go on in the course
he was pursuing, assuring him that there was
mercy for the vilest of sinners if penitent, which
afforded him great consolation.

Nevertheless   the   remorse-stricken   sinner
considered that his misdeeds had been such that
he could scarcely do sufficient in the way of
mortification to obliterate the guilt of the past,
and he determined upon withdrawing himself
entirely from communion with his fellow-
creatures, even from the Holy Brotherhood of
Whitby, and devote the remainder of his life to
meditation and prayer altogether apart from the
world.

Connected with the Abbey there was, in a

solitary place of the forest which fringed the banks of the Esk, a chapel where the monks were wont to retire at certain seasons for the purpose of devotion, away from the bustle and distraction inevitable in a large community ; and in close proximity to this chapel, Jerome built for himself a wooden hut in which to pass his remaining years as a hermit, secluded from society, living on wild fruit and roots, quenching his thirst from the streamlet which trickled past, and spending his days and nights in prayer, flagellation, and abstinence.

Resident in the neighbourhood of Whitby were two landed proprietors—Ralph de Perci, Lord of Sneton, and William de Brus, Lord of Ugglebarnby, who were great lovers of hunting and other field sports, and near them lived one Allatson, a gentleman and freeholder. The three were boon companions, and constantly meeting in the pursuance of country sports, and at each other's houses for the purpose of carousing together. One night when they were thus assembled together they arranged to go boar-hunting on the following day, which was the 16th of October, 5th Henry II., in the forest of Eskdale ; and soon after dinner they met, attired in their hunting garbs, with boar-staves in their hands, and accompanied by a pack of boar-hounds, yelping and barking, and as eager for the sport as their masters.

A boar was soon started, which plunged into the recesses of the forest, followed by the hounds in full cry, and by the hunters, shouting to encourage them. Onward they rushed, through brake and briar, the huge animal clearing a pathway through the tangled underwood, which enabled his pursuers to follow without much impediment. Onward they went in hot speed, the hounds sometimes overtaking the boar, and tearing him with their fangs, and the hunters beating him with their staves, maddening him with rage, and causing him to turn upon his pursuers, and rend the dogs with his fangs, as he would also the hunters, could he have escaped the environment of the dogs; and then he would dash onward again, evidently becoming more and more exhausted from wounds and bruises and loss of blood, until at length they came in sight of the chapel and hermitage; from which point we cannot do better than continue the narrative in the words of Burton, as given in his " Monasticon Ebor."

" The boar," says he, " being very sore and very hotly pursued, and dead run, took in at the chapel door and there died, whereof the hermit shut the hounds out of the chapel and kept himself within at his meditations, the hounds standing at bay without.

" The gentlemen called to the hermit (Brother Jerome), who opened the door. They found the boar dead, for which they, in very great fury (because their hounds were put from their game) did, most violently and cruelly, run at the hermit with their boar staves, whereby he died soon after."

Fearful of the consequences of their crime, they fled to Scarborough, and took sanctuary in the church ; but the Abbot of Whitby, who was a friend of the King, was authorised to take them out, " whereby they came in danger of the law, and not to be privileged, but likely to have the severity of the law, which was death."

The hermit, who had been brought to Whitby Abbey, lay at the point of death when the prisoners were brought thither ; and hearing of their arrival, he besought the Abbot that they might be brought into his presence ; and when they made their appearance said to them, " I am

o

sure to die of these wounds you gave me."
"Aye," quoth the Abbot, "and they shall surely
die for the same." "Not so," continued the
dying man, " for I will freely forgive them my
death if they will be contented to be enjoined
this penance for the safeguard of their souls."
"Enjoin what penance you will," replied the
culprits, "so that you save our lives." Then
Brother Jerome explained the nature of the
penance :—" You and yours shall hold your lands
of the Abbot of Whitby and his successors in this
manner. That upon Ascension Eve, you, or
some of you, shall come to the woods of Stray-
heads, which is in Eskdale, the same day at
sunrising, and there shall the abbot's officer blow
his horn, to the intent that you may know how
to find him ; and he shall deliver unto you,
William de Brus, ten stakes, eleven strutstowers,
and eleven yethers, to be cut by you, or some of
you, with a knife of one penny price ; and you,
Ralph de Perci, shall take twenty and one of
each sort, to be cut in the same manner ; and
you, Allatson, shall take nine of each sort to be
cut as aforesaid, and to be taken on your backs
and carried to the town of Whitby, and to be
there before nine of the clock the same day

before mentioned. If at the same hour of nine
of the clock it be full sea, your labour or service
shall cease; but if it be not full sea, each of you
shall set your stakes at the brim and so yether
them, on each side of your yethers, and so stake
on each side with your strowers, that they may
stand three tides, without removing by the force
thereof. Each of you shall make and execute the
said service at that very hour, every year, except
it shall be full sea at that hour; but when it shall
so fall out, this service shall cease. . . . You
shall faithfully do this, in remembrance that you
did most cruelly slay me; and that you may the
better call to God for mercy, repent unfeignedly
for your sins, and do good works. The officer of
Eskdale side shall blow—'Out on you! out on
you! out on you!' for this heinous crime. If
you, or your successors, shall refuse this service,
so long as it shall not be full sea, at the aforesaid
hour, you, or yours, shall forfeit your lands to
the Abbot of Whitby, or his successors. This I
entreat, and earnestly beg that you may have
lives and goods preserved for this service; and
I request of you to promise, by your parts in
Heaven, that it shall be done by you and your
successors as it is aforesaid requested, and I will

confirm it by the faith of an honest man." Then the hermit said, "My soul longeth for the Lord; and I do freely forgive these men my death, as Christ forgave the thief upon the cross," and in the presence of the Abbot and the rest, he said, moreover, these words, "In manas tuas, domine, commendo spiritum, meum, avinculis enim mortis redemisti me Domine veritatis. Amen." So he yielded up the ghost the 8th day of December, A.D. 1160, upon whose soul God have mercy. Amen.

In 1753, the service was rendered by the last of the Allatsons, the Lords of Sneton and Ugglebarnby having, it is supposed, bought off their share of the penance. He held a piece of land, of £10 a year, at Fylingdales, for which he brought five stakes, eight yethers, and six strutstowers, and whilst Mr. Cholmley's bailiff, on an antique bugle horn, blew "out on you," he made a slight edge of them a little way into the shallow of the river.

Burton, writing in 1757, adds, "This little farm is now out of the Allatson family, but the present owner performed the service last Ascension Eve, A.D. 1756."

The horn garth or yether hedge, as the fence

was called, was constructed yearly on the east side of the Esk for the purpose of keeping cattle from the landing places.

Charlton, in his history of Whitby, discredits this tradition, saying that there were no such persons as those mentioned, and no chapel, only a hermitage in the forest ; that the making of the horn garth is of much older date than that indicated, and that there is no record in the annals of the abbey of its ever having been made by way of penance ; concluding that it is altogether a monkish invention.

The Calverley Ghost.

LITTLE northward of the road from Bradford to Leeds, four miles distant from the former and seven from the latter, lies the village of Calverley, the seat of a knightly family of that name for some 600 years. They occupied a stately mansion, which was converted into workmen's tenements early in the present century, and the chapel transformed into a wheelwright's shop.

Near by is a lane, a weird and lonesome road a couple of centuries ago, overshadowed as it was by trees, which cast a ghostly gloom over it after the setting of the sun. It was not much frequented excepting in broad daylight, and even then only by the bolder and more stout-hearted of the village rustics, whilst the majority would as soon have dared to sleep in the charnel-house under the church as have passed down it by night, or even in the gloaming. Instances were known of strangers having unwittingly gone through it, all of whom, however, came forth with trembling limbs and scared faces, their hair erect on their heads, and the perspiration streaming down from their foreheads. When questioned as to what they had seen, the reply was always the same, a cloud-like apparition, thin, transparent, and unsubstantial, bearing the semblance of a human figure, with no seeming clothing, but simply a misty, impalpable shape ; the features frenzied with rage and madness, and in the right hand the appearance of a bloody dagger. The apparition, they averred, seemed to consolidate into form out of a mist which environed them soon after entering the lane, and continued to accompany them, but without sound, sign, or motion, save that of gliding along, accommodating itself to the pace of the terrified passenger, which was usually that of a full run, until the other end of the lane was reached, when it melted again into a mere shapeless mass of vapour.

The apparition was that of the disquieted soul of a certain Walter Calverley, which was denied the calm repose of death, and condemned to flit about this lane, as a penance for a great and unnatural crime of which he had been guilty.

Various attempts were made to exorcise the restless spirit, but all were ineffectual until some very potent spiritual agencies were employed, which were successful in "laying the ghost," but only for a time, as they operate only so long as a certain holly tree, planted by the hand of the delinquent, continues to flourish, when that decays the ghost may again be looked for.

The Calverleys (originally Scott) were a family of distinction in Yorkshire from the time of Henry I. to the period of the great Civil War, intermarrying with some of the best families, and producing a succession of notable men.

John Scott was steward to Maud, daughter of Malcolm Canmore, King of Scotland, and niece of Edgar the Atheling, the last scion of the Saxon race of English Kings; he accompanied her to England on the occasion of her alliance with King Henry I., and married Larderina, daughter of Alphonsus Gospatrick, Lord of Calverley and other Yorkshire manors, who was descended from Gospatrick, Earl of Northumbria, who so stoutly supported the claims of Edgar the Atheling to the crown of England in opposition to that of the usurping conqueror, William the

Norman. By this marriage, John Scott became *j.u.* Lord of Calverley.

William, his grandson, gave the vicarage of Calverley to the chantry of the Blessed Virgin, York Cathedral, *temp.* Henry III.

John, his descendant, in the fourteenth century, assumed the name of de Calverley in lieu of Scott.

Sir John, Knight, his son, had issue three sons and a daughter, Isabel, who became Prioress of Esholt.

John, his son, was one of the squires to Anne, Queen of Richard II. He fought in the French wars, was captured there, and beheaded for some "horrible crime, the particulars of which are not known," and dying *cæl*, was succeeded by his brother, Walter, whose second son, Sir Walter, was instrumental in the rebuilding of the church of Calverley, and caused his arms—six owls—to be carved on the woodwork.

Sir John, Knight, his son, was created a Knight-Banneret, and slain at Shrewsbury, 1403, fighting under the banner of Henry IV. against the Percies. Dying *s.p.*, his brother Walter succeeded, whose second son, Thomas, was ancestor, by his wife, Agnes Scargill, of the

Calverleys of Morley and of county Cumberland.

Sir William, his grandson, was created a Knight-Banneret for valour in the Scottish wars, by the Earl of Surrey ; his grandson, Sir William Knight, was Sheriff of Yorkshire, and died 1571 ; Thomas, his second son, was ancestor of the Calverleys of county Durham. Sir Walter, his son, had issue three sons, of whom Edmund, the third, was ancestor of the Calverleys of counties Sussex and Surrey.

William, the eldest son of Sir Walter, whose portrait was exhibited at York in 1868, married Catherine, daughter of Sir John Thornholm, Knight, of Haysthorpe, near Bridlington. This lady was a devoted Catholic, and suffered much persecution for adhering to her faith and giving refuge to proscribed priests, the estates being sequestered and some manors sold to pay the fine for recusancy. They had issue Walter, the subject of this tradition.

Walter Calverley was born in the reign of Elizabeth, and in his youth witnessed the relentless persecutions which his family, being adherents of the old faith, had to endure from the ascendant Protestantism, which held the reins of govern-

ment. Those of the reformed religion were wont
to style Mary the "Bloody Queen," for the
number of executions and barbarities which, in
the name of religion, stained the annals of her
reign ; but it was a notable instance of the pot-
and-kettle style of vituperation, as the burning
and hanging and quartering and pressing to death
of Jesuits and seminary priests, and of lay men
and women who afforded them refuge, went on
as merrily during the reigns of her two following
successors, as did the roasting of heretics at
Smithfield and elsewhere under Bonner and
Gardiner. He was witness, when a boy, of the
barbarous treatment to which his mother was
subjected for worshipping God according to the
dictates of her conscience and for daring to shelter
priests of her persuasion.

Walter was a lad of strong passions and
vehement spirit, and the sight of the sufferings
endured by the friends and co-religionists of his
family drove him almost to madness. He would
stamp his foot, clench his fist, and vow vengeance
upon the perpetrators, and it is highly probable
that he consorted and plotted with Guy Fawkes
and others of the gunpowder conspirators at
Scotton, near Knaresborough, and might have

had a hand in the great plot itself, which culminated and collapsed in the same year that he committed the crime which cost him his life.

He married Philippa, daughter of the Hon. Henry Brooke, fifth son of George, fourth Baron Cobham, and sister of John, first Baron of the second creation, and by her had issue three sons, the third of whom, Henry, succeeded to the estates, whose son, Sir Walter, was a great sufferer in person and estate for his loyalty during the Civil War, and who was father of Sir Walter, who was created a baronet by Queen Anne in 1711, the title becoming extinct in 1777, on the death, without surviving issue, of his son, Sir Walter Calverley-Blackett.

For a few years the newly-married couple lived in tolerable harmony and happiness, such as falls to the lot of most married people. They looked forward to giving an heir to the family estates who should perpetuate the name in lineal descent ; but the months and years passed by, and they began to experience the truth that " hope deferred maketh the heart sick," as no heir made his appearance, which was an especial disappointment to the Lord of the Calverley domain, and gave rise to the idea that he had married one

who was barren, and incapable of giving him an
heir. Brooding over this impediment to his
hopes, he grew moody and discontented; treated
his wife not only with neglect, but upbraided her
with opprobrious epithets, treated her with cold
and cruel disfavour, and in his occasional violent
outbursts of passion would wish her dead, that
he might marry again to a more fruitful wife.
Moreover he gave way to over-indulgence in
deep potations of ale, sack, and " distilled waters,"
which added fire and force to his naturally fierce
temperament, and rendered him almost maniacal
in his acts. He was profuse in his hospitality
to his neighbours, frequently giving dinner
parties to his roystering friends, with whom he
would sit until late in the night, or rather until
early in the morning carousing over their cups.

Amongst the friends who thus visited him was
a certain country squire of the name of Leventhorpe, a young fellow of handsome figure and
insinuating address, who would drink his bottle
with the veriest toper, and yet would conduct
himself in the company of ladies with the utmost
decorum and most fascinating demeanour, would
converse with them on flowers and birds and
tapestry work, and quote with admirable ac-

centuation and feeling passages from the writings of the popular poets, or recite with pathos and humour the novelettes of the Italian romancists, which then were the delight of every lady's boudoir. He was introduced by Calverley to his wife, and she being naturally of a lively, vivacious disposition, and, like ladies of the present age, a passionate admirer of works of fiction and imagination, she took great pleasure in his society, as, indeed, he did in hers, and he was consequently a constant visitor at Calverley Hall, whether invited or not, and whether the lady's husband was at home or not; but always was he gladly welcome, and in pure innocence and without any idea of impropriety, by the lady. On his side, too, he went to the house as a man might do to that of a sister, without any sentiment save that of friendship, or, at the utmost, a feeling of platonic love. Not so, however, the lady's husband. He began to feel annoyed and disquieted at witnessing their growing intimacy, but hitherto saw no reason to doubt the fidelity of his wife. Some twelve months after the introduction of Leventhorpe to the Hall, symptoms became evident of the probable birth of a child, and Calverley at first hailed the prospect with satisfaction, praying and hoping that it might prove to be the long-wished-for son and heir. In due course the child was born, and of the desired sex, and great were the rejoicings and splendid the banqueting at the christening. The next year a second son made his appearance, and then dark thoughts and suspicions began to flit across Calverley's mind. He considered it strange that no child should have been born during the early years of his marriage, but that immediately after Leventhorpe's introduction to the house his wife began to prove fruitful, and had borne two children, with the prospect of a third. He brooded over these dark thoughts by night and day until they ripened into positive jealousy and the belief that the children were Leventhorpe's, and not his own.

Influenced by these sentiments, he drank still more deeply, and was frequently subjected to *delirium tremens* and maniacal fits of passion, which rendered him the terror of all by whom he was surrounded. He could not openly accuse Leventhorpe of a breach of the seventh commandment, of which he believed him guilty, as he had no basis of fact upon which to ground the charge; but he found means to quarrel with him on some frivolous point, and made use of such expressions of vituperation as he thought would impel him to demand satisfaction at the sword's point; but Leventhorpe was a quiet, peaceable man, who swallowed the affront, attributing it to the deranged state of his friend's mind, induced by too free application to the bottle; and he simply abstained from visiting the house.

"He is a coward as well as a knave," said Calverley to himself. "No gentleman would listen to such language as I have used and submit to it patiently like a beaten cur, without resenting it with his sword, and this circumstance proves his guilt, and the certainty of my suspicions; but I will be amply revenged on both him and his paramour and their progeny;" and he drank and drank day after day, and more and more deeply, until he at length brought himself to a state fitting him for a madhouse and personal restraint. Many a time he sought for Leventhorpe, with the hope of provoking him to fight, but was not able to accomplish his purpose, as circumstances had called Leventhorpe to London, where he remained some months.

In the meantime the third child was born,

and as the mother's health was delicate, it was sent out to nurse at a farm-house some two or three miles distant, and it was then that Calverley charged his wife, to her face, with adultery, adding that he felt positively assured that the children were Leventhorpe's. She indignantly repelled the charge, assuring him, with an appeal to the Virgin Mary as to the truth of what she was saying, that the children were his and nobody else's; but he would not listen to her denials—called her tears, which were flowing profusely, the hypocritical tears of a strumpet, and cursed and swore at her, threatening a dire vengeance on her and her seducer, and finally left her in a fit of hysterics in the hands of her women, who had rushed in on hearing her screams. He then went downstairs to his dining room and sat down to dinner, but could not eat much, each mouthful as he swallowed it seeming as if it would choke him. "Take these things away," he exclaimed in a furious tone to his servants, "and bring me sack, and plenty of it." The terrified menials saw that he was in one of his maniacal moods, and knew that it would be aggravated by drinking, but dared not disobey him. The sack was placed on the

P

table, and he dismissed the attendants with a curse. Flagon after flagon he poured out and drank in rapid succession, which soon produced its natural effect. "Ah, demon!" said he, "have you come again to torment me? Why sit you there, opposite me, grinning and gesticulating? You are an ugly devil, sure enough, with your fiery eyes, your pointed horns, and your barbed tail. You tell me that it were but just to murder my wife, Leventhorpe, and their brats, and I don't know but what the advice is good. Aye, twirl your tail as a dog does when he is pleased; you think you have got another recruit for your nether kingdom, and you are right. I live here a hell upon earth, and I do not see that I shall be much the worse off with you below; besides I shall have the satisfaction of vengeance, and that will repay me amply for any after-death punishment. Aye, grin on, but leave me now to finish this bottle in quietness, for I cannot drink with comfort whilst you are grimacing and jibing at me there." He spoke this in a loud tone of voice, to which the scared servants were listening at the door, after which he continued to drain goblet after goblet, giving forth utterances more and more incoherent, until at length he fell from his chair with a heavy thump on the floor. Hearing this, the servants entered, and found him, as they had often found him before, in a state of senseless intoxication, and carried him up to bed.

Having slept off his debauch, he awoke late the following morning with a raging thirst, which he endeavoured to assuage by deep draughts of ale. Breakfast he could eat none, but continued drinking until his familiar demon again made his appearance, and seemed to incite him to the fulfilment of his vow of revenge. Leventhorpe was out of his reach, but the other destined victims were at hand, and what more fitting time than the present for the execution of his purpose? He selected a dagger from his store of weapons, and carefully sharpened it to a fine point; then gave directions to have his horse saddled and brought to the door of the hall to await his pleasure. As he had three or four men-servants, who might hinder him in his intent, he sent them on several errands about the estate, and when they had departed, leaving only the female domestics in the house, he went, dagger in hand, into the hall, where he found his eldest son playing. Seizing him by the hair of his head, he stabbed him in three or four places, and, taking him in his arms, carried him bleeding to his mother's apartment. " There," said he, throwing the body down, " is one of the fruits of your illicit intercourse, and the others must share the same fate." So saying, he laid hold of his second son, who was in the room, and stabbed him to the heart. The mother, shrieking with terror and agony, rushed forward to save the child, but was too late, and herself received three or four blows from the dagger, and fell senseless to the floor, but more from horror and fright than from her wounds, which were but slight, thanks to a steel stomacher which she wore. Imagining that he had killed her as well as the children, he mounted his horse and rode towards the village, where his youngest child was at nurse, with the intention of killing it also, but on the road he was thrown from his horse, and before he could re-mount was secured by his servants, who had gone in pursuit of him.

He was taken before the nearest magistrate— Sir John Bland, of Kippax—and in the course of his examination stated that he had meditated the deed for four years, and that he was fully convinced that the children were not his. He was committed to York Castle and brought to trial, but refusing to plead, was subjected to *peine forte et dure.* He was taken to the press-yard, stripped to his shirt, and laid on a board with a stone under his back; his arms were stretched out and secured by cords; another board was placed over his body, upon which were laid heavy weights one by one, he being asked in the intervals if he still refused. He bore the agony with firmness and endurance, even when the great pressure broke his ribs and caused them to protrude from the sides. As weight after weight was added, nothing could be extorted from him save groans caused by the intensity of the pain, which at length ceased and the weights were removed, revealing a mere mass of crushed bloody flesh and mangled bones.

The two children died, and the third lived to succeed to the estates. The mother also recovered, and married for her second husband Sir Thomas Burton, Knight.

"Two Most Unnatural and Bloodie Murthers, by Master Calverley, a Yorkshire gentleman, upon his wife and two children, 1605." Edited by J. Payne Collier, 1863.

"A Yorkshire Tragedy, not so new as lamentable, by Mr. Shakespeare ; acted at the Globe, 1608. London 1619. With a portrait of the brat at nurse." Attributed to Shakespeare (without proof) by Stevens and others.

" The Fatal Extravagance. By Joseph Mitchell, 1720." A play based on the same subject, and performed at the Lincoln's Inn Theatre.

The incident is also introduced by Harrison Ainsworth in his romance of " Rookwood."

The Bewitched House of Wakefield.

IN the earlier half of the seventeenth century, and during the Commonwealth, there dwelt in a mud-walled and thatched cottage, in the environs of Wakefield, a "wise woman," as she was styled, named Jennet Benton, with her son, George Benton. He had been a soldier in the Parliamentarian army, but, since its disbandment, had loafed about Wakefield without any ostensible occupation, living, as it appeared, on his mother's earnings in her profession. As a "wise woman," she was resorted to by great numbers of people —by persons who had lost property, to gain a clue to the discovery of the pilferers—by men to learn the most propitious times for harvesting, sheepshearing, etc.—by matrons to obtain charms for winning back their dissipated or unfaithful husbands to domestic life, as it existed the first few months after marriage—and by young men and maidens for consultation with her on matters of love ; and, as no advice was given without its equivalent in the coin of the realm, she made a very fair living, and was enabled to maintain her son in idleness, who was wont to spend a great part of his time in pot houses, with other quondam troopers, their chief topics of discourse being disputed points of controversy between the Independents and Presbyterians, and revilings of the Popish whore of Babylon and her progeny, the Church of England. Although not imbued with much of the spirit of piety, Benton, in his campaigning career, had imbibed much of the fanaticism, superstition, and phraseology of the lower class of the Puritans, such of them as assumed the hypocritical garb of Puritanism to curry favour with their superiors, who were, as a rule, men of sincere piety, and, in so doing, somewhat overdid the part by altogether out-Puritaning them in the extravagance of their outbursts of zeal, and in the almost blasphemous use of Scriptural expressions. Such was Benton amongst his companions, and he passed for a fairly godly man. With his mother, however, he cast off all this assumption of religion and the use of Bible phrases, for she was a woman who despised all religions alike, and sneered equally at

the "snivelling cant" of the Puritans, the proud
arrogance of the Bishops of the Church, and the
" absurd drivellings" of the Separatists; but
these ideas she was sufficiently wise to keep to
herself, or confide them to her son alone. She
even went occasionally to church and conventicle,
that she might stand well with her customers,
who were of all sects. She had, besides, a
voluble tongue, and was not deficient in in-
telligence, so that she was able to converse with
all, each one according to his doctrinal bias, so as
to leave an impression that she was not opposed
but rather inclined to the particular theological
dogma then under discussion.

There was, however, a vague idea prevalent in
Wakefield that Mother Benton was a witch, had
intercourse with the Devil, and was a dangerous
person to deal with otherwise than on friendly
terms. She was old, wrinkled, and ungainly in
features; unmistakable characteristics of the
sisterhood. She was possessed of wisdom in
occult matters seemingly superhuman, which
could only be derived from a compact with Satan.
She had a huge black cat, presumably an imp,
her familiar, who would bristle up his hair and
spit viciously at the old woman's visitors until

restrained by her command. On one occasion, however, a handsome young man came from her cottage followed by the cat, which was observed to purr and rub himself affectionately against his legs, who, it was assumed, could be none other· than the Father of Evil himself, who had assumed that guise to pay a friendly visit to his servant and disciple. She was also sometimes away from her cottage for a night, and the inquiry arose— for what purpose, excepting to attend a Sabbath of the witches. It is true she had never been seen passing through the air astride of her broom, but it was noticed that whenever she was absent on such occasions her broom, which usually stood outside her cottage door, disappeared also, and was found in its place again on her return.

At this time the belief in witchcraft was universally prevalent, as we find in the narrative of the witches of Fuystone, in the forest of Knaresborough, who played such pranks in the family of Edward Fairfax, the translator of Tasso, about the same time. Indeed it was considered as impious then to doubt their existence as it is nowadays of their master and instigator, for is there not a Scriptural precept—" Thou shalt not suffer a witch to live ? " and was there not a witch of Endor who summoned the spirit of Samuel? Besides, had not many decrepit half-witted old women, when subjected to torture, confessed that they had entered into compact with the Devil, bargaining their souls for length of years and the power of inflicting mischief on their neighbours? It is quite certain that the evidences of Mother Benton being one of the sisterhood of Satan were so palpable that had she not been so useful in Wakefield in her vocation of a "wise woman" she would have been subjected to the usual ordeal, by way of testing whether she were a witch or not. This ordeal consisted of stripping the accused, tying her thumbs to her great toes and throwing her into a pond : if she floated, it was a proof that she, having rejected the baptismal water of regeneration, the water rejected her, and she was hauled out and burnt at the stake as an undoubted witch, but if she sank and were drowned she was declared innocent ; so that, were she guilty or innocent of the foul crime, the result was pretty much the same, excepting in the mode of terminating her existence.

At this time one Richard Jackson held a farm called Bunny Hall, under a Mr. Stringer, of Sharlston, which lay near to Jennet Benton's cottage. Over one of Jackson's fields was a pathway, really for the use of the tenant of the farm, but which was used on sufferance by others, Jennet and her son frequently having occasion to pass along it. Jackson, however, in consequence of the damage done to his crops by passengers, disputed the right of the public, and issued a public notice that after a certain date it would be closed. The people of Wakefield, in reply to the notice, asserted that it was an ancient footpath that had belonged to the public time out of mind, and that they intended to continue the use of it in spite of Jackson's prohibition. Jennet and her son were the ring-leaders of this opposition, and after the closure of the path, passed over the railings placed across the entrance, and were going along as they had been wont to do, when they were met by Daniel Craven, one of Jackson's servants, who told them that they could not be allowed to cross the field as it was private property. An angry altercation ensued, in the course of which George Benton took up a piece of flint and threw it with great force at Craven, " wherewith he cut his over-lipp and broake two teeth out of his chaps," and thus having overcome their opponent they went onward and out at the other end. An action for trespass was then laid against George Benton by Farmer Jackson, who appears to have won his cause, as Benton "submitted to it, and indevors were used to end the difference, which was composed and satisfaction given unto the said Craven;" satisfaction of a pecuniary nature, no doubt.

A few days after the judicial termination of the case, "Jackson *v.* Benton," the farmer was riding home from Wakefield market. He had to pass Jennet's cottage on his road, and he thought to accost her in a conciliatory style, as he did not wish to be at variance with his neighbours, especially with one who had the reputation of being "a wise woman," whose services he might require in cases of pilfering, sheep stealing, and the like; in cases of sickness amongst his children, or a murrain amongst his cattle; or in other cases beyond the ken of ordinary mortals; hence he considered it politic to remain on good terms with her, although he had felt it his duty to maintain the action for trespass.

As he approached the cottage, the old woman was seated outside her door, watching a cauldron suspended from cross sticks, in which was simmering a decoction of herbs, to eventuate in a love philtre probably for some love-sick maiden. By her side was seated her black cat, who bridled up and spat viciously at the farmer as he came up.

"Ah, mother Benton," said he, reining up, "busy as usual, I see, preparing something for the benefit of one of your clients."

"It is no business of yours what I am preparing," she replied. "I sent not for you, nor do I want your conversation or interference in my concerns. Go your way, or it may be the worse for you."

"Nay, good dame, be not angry, I came not to interfere with your concerns; I merely stopped on my road home to say 'good even' to you, and to see if I could be of any service to you, for I desire to cultivate the good-will of my neighbours."

"And a pretty way you have of doing so by prosecuting them in law courts for maintaining the rights of themselves and their ancestors for generations past."

"That I was compelled to do, good Jennet, for the maintenance of my own rights. It was a necessity forced upon me, but I bear no ill-will to either you or your son. And see, as a proof thereof, I have brought you a new kirtle from Wakefield," at the same time drawing from his saddlebags a flaming scarlet garment of that kind, which he threw into her lap.

"Farmer Jackson," said she, "come not here with your honied lips and deceitful expressions of friendship. I want none of your gifts," and taking up the kirtle, she rent it into a dozen pieces, and thrust them into the fire under the cauldron.

"Listen to me one moment," commenced Jackson, but the old beldame, rising up into a majestic attitude, interrupted him with, "I will listen no more to your hypocritical palaver. You have done me a grievous wrong in citing my son before your law courts, it is an unpardonable offence, and soon shall you know what it is to incur the wrath of Jennet Benton, the wise woman of Wakefield. Within a twelvemonth and a day, Farmer Jackson, shall you find at what cost you set the myrmidons of the law upon me and my belongings, and from that time to your life's end shall you rue that day's work. It is I, the wise woman of Wakefield, who say it, and see if I am not a true soothsayer, and merit the appellation I bear. That is all I have got to say," and she passed into her cottage, whilst the farmer rode homeward, not without a foreboding of impending evil.

We have many narratives on record of houses that have been the scenes of remarkable disturbances and strange apparitions, of furniture moved from place to place without apparent agency, of domestic utensils thrown about by no perceptible impelling power, and of noises attributable to no human cause, problems that in many cases have never been solved, but which have usually been ascribed to some mischievous goblin, or to the ghost of some unhappy person who has come by death unfairly and by foul means.

Farmer Jackson's house and homestead from this time, for the period of a year and a day, became haunted in this fashion, but here there could be no doubt as to the cause. It was the spell cast over it by the machinations of the witch, Jennet Benton, and it was in fact not a haunted but a bewitched house.

As Jackson rode home he thought of the curse laid upon him by the witch, but being a strong-minded man he did not entertain the current

superstition as to the superhuman diabolic power
said to be possessed by such persons, and he felt
little or no apprehension on that score; yet he
inclined so far to the popular belief as to fear that
by some means she might cast incantations over
his cattle and crops, so as to cause the former to
sicken and die, and the latter to wither and come
to naught.

On reaching his home he stabled his horse, and
going indoors he accosted his wife with some
cursory remark, but she made no reply, and he
thought to himself, " She is sullen to-night—
in one of her tantrums; what's the matter, I
wonder." He then sat down to supper, with his
children about him, and a couple of maid-servants
employed in some domestic duty, when his wife
inquired, " Why are you all so silent; are you all
dumb; have you got anything to tell me about
the doings at the market, husband, goodman?"
" What on earth do you mean?" inquired
Jackson; " I spoke to you when I came in, and
there has been noise enough among the children
since then to waken the Seven Sleepers." Mrs.
Jackson still stood staring, with a vacant
countenance, and said, after a pause, " Why don't
you reply? It seems as if one were in the

charnel-house of the church, surrounded by the
dead." It then occurred to Jackson that his wife
must have suddenly become stone deaf, and by
means of signs and such writing as the family had
at command, he ascertained that such was the
fact; but he dreamt not that it was the beginning
of the witch's spell.

A night or two after, one of the children was
stricken by an epileptic fit, throwing itself about
with great violence and twisting its body with
strange contortions, with convulsive writhings,
and requiring to be held down by three or four
persons to prevent its doing itself an injury.

One morning the swineherd of the farm came
into the room where Jackson was sitting at
breakfast, and with a scared countenance told him
that a herd of swine that had been shut up in
a barn the previous night "had broake thorrow
two barn dores," and had fled no one knew
whither. A search was immediately instituted,
but it was not until after two or three days that
a portion of the herd was found at a considerable
distance from the farm, the remainder being lost
altogether.

On another occasion Jackson himself, "although
helthfull of body, was suddenly taken without any

probable reason to be given or naturall cause appearing, being sometimes in such extremity that he conceived himselfe drawne in pieces at the hart, backe, and shoulders." During the first fit he heard the sound of music and dancing, as if in the room where he lay. He partially recovered the following day, but at twelve o'clock the next night he had another fit, and during its continuance he heard a loud ringing of bells, accompanied by sounds of singing and dancing. He inquired of his wife, who appears by this time to have recovered her sense of hearing, what the bell-ringing and singing meant; but she replied that she heard nothing of it, as also did his man. "He asked them againe and againe if they heard it not. At last he and his wife and servant heard it (what?) give three hevie groones. At that instant doggs did howle and yell at the windows as though they would heve puld them in pieces."

Jackson now became fully convinced that he was enduring all these trials and sufferings from the curse of the witch Jennet, and he expressed this opinion to his friends who came to condole with him. They, with neighbourly feeling, proposed to put the question to the test by submitting the old woman to the usual ordeal of the horse pond; but he would not hear of this, not even yet, with such probable evidence, believing that Satan could be authorised to endow old women with such mischievous powers. By the counsel of his friends, however, he sanctioned the sending a deputation to Jennet to investigate the matter. The deputation went to her cottage and told her their errand, but she only laughed at them. "It is true," said she, "that I called down the wrath of Heaven upon him and his belongings for his cruel persecution of a helpless widow and her orphan son; and if God has listened to my supplication, and sent calamity upon him, it is intended as a warning to him that, for the future, he may be more merciful to the poor and unprotected. If he chooses to blame any one, he must attribute his punishment to a much higher power than a feeble mortal such as I am."

During all this time Jackson's house was rendered almost uninhabitable by noises and apparitions, so that the servants fled from it panic-stricken, and others could not be found to take their places. The commencement of the disturbances was some six months after the utterance of the curse. The family were seated at supper when a tremendous crash was heard in the next room, as if some heavy metal vessel had been flung violently on the floor. Supposing it to be something that had fallen from a shelf or a hook in the ceiling, they went into the room, but found nothing to account for the noise. At other times it would seem as if all the doors of the house were being slammed to, or the windows shaken as by a storm of wind, although there was not the slightest agitation in the atmosphere. Then would occur shrieks as of persons in distress, groans as of sufferers in agonies of pain, and bursts of demoniac laughter, with a flapping of huge bat-like wings. "Apparitions like blacke dogges and catts were also scene," which darted out from under the furniture and usually passed out up the chimney, it being immaterial whether or not a fire was blazing in the grate. Along with all these disturbances in the house and unaccountable illnesses of the various members of the household, the horses and cattle of the farm were subjected to similar inflictions, much to the detriment of Jackson's material prosperity. Week after week news came in of the death of horses, cows, and sheep : and in his deposition at York, Jackson said that "since the time the said Jennet and George Benton threatened him he hath lost eighteen horses and meares, and he conceives he hath had all this loss by the use of some witchcraft or sorcerie by the said Jennet and George Benton."

For a twelvemonth and a day these disturbances, sufferings, and losses continued, rendering Jackson almost bankrupt, and then they all at once ceased.

Being fully convinced that these troubles had been caused by the diabolical incantations of the witch Jennet, he brought a charge against her and her son, at York, of practising witchcraft against him, and they were tried at the assizes on the 7th June, 1656. The depositions of the trial are printed in a volume published by the Surtees Society in 1861, entitled "Depositions from the Castle of York relating to offences committed in the northern counties during the seventeenth century. Edited by J. Raine."

YORKSHIRE FAMILY ROMANCE.

By FREDERICK ROSS, F.R.H.S.

AUTHOR OF "THE RUINED ABBEYS OF ENGLAND," "CELEBRITIES OF
YORKSHIRE WOLDS," "BIOGRAPHIA EBORACENSIS,"
"THE PROGRESS OF CIVILISATION," ETC.

AMONGST Yorkshire Authors Mr. FREDERICK ROSS
occupies a leading place. For over sixty years he has
been a close student of the history of his native
county, and perhaps no author has written so much and well
respecting it. His residence in London has enabled him to
take advantage of the important stores of unpublished information contained in the British Museum, the Public Record
Office, and in other places. He has also frequently visited
Yorkshire to collect materials for his works. His new book
is one of the most readable and instructive he has written.
It will be observed from the following list of subjects that the
work is of wide and varied interest, and makes a permanent
contribution to Yorkshire literature.

CONTENTS:

IMPORTANT NOTICE.—The Edition is limited to 500 copies,
and the greater part are sold. The book will advance
in price in course of time.

HULL: WILLIAM ANDREWS & CO., THE HULL PRESS.
London: Simpkin, Marshall, Hamilton, Kent, & Co., Ltd.

Elegantly bound in cloth gilt, demy 8vo., price 6s.

𝕺𝖑𝖉 𝕮𝖍𝖚𝖗𝖈𝖍 𝕷𝖔𝖗𝖊.

By WILLIAM ANDREWS, F.R.H.S.,

*Author of "Curiosities of the Church," "Old-Time Punishments,"
"Historic Romance," etc.*

CONTENTS.

The Right of Sanctuary—The Romance of Trial—A Fight between the Mayor of Hull and the Archbishop of York—Chapels on Bridges—Charter Horns—The Old English Sunday—The Easter Sepulchre—St. Paul's Cross—Cheapside Cross—The Biddenden Maids Charity—Plagues and Pestilences—A King Curing an Abbot of Indigestion—The Services and Customs of Royal Oak Day—Marrying in a White Sheet—Marrying under the Gallows—Kissing the Bride—Hot Ale at Weddings—Marrying Children—The Passing Bell—Concerning Coffins—The Curfew Bell—Curious Symbols of the Saints—Acrobats on Steeples—A carefully-prepared Index.

ILLUSTRATED.

PRESS OPINIONS.

"A worthy work on a deeply interesting subject. We commend this book strongly."—*European Mail.*

"An interesting volume."—*The Scotsman.*

"Contains much that will interest and instruct."—*Glasgow Herald.*

"Mr. Andrews' book does not contain a dull page. . . . Deserves to meet with a very warm welcome."—*Yorkshire Post.*

"Mr. Andrews, in 'Old Church Lore,' makes the musty parchments and records he has consulted redolent with life and actuality, and has added to his works a most interesting volume, which, written in a light and easy narrative style, is anything but of the 'dry-as-dust' order. The book is handsomely got up, being both bound and printed in an artistic fashion."—*Northern Daily News.*

HULL : WILLIAM ANDREWS & CO., THE HULL PRESS.
London : Simpkin, Marshall, Hamilton, Kent, & Co., Ltd.

www.ingramcontent.com/pod-product-compliance
Lightning Source LLC
Chambersburg PA
CBHW022006050726
47499CB00006BB/1757